GLASS
secrets

BOOK 2 OF THE *SHATTERED COVE* SERIES

A. M. KUSI

Published by A. M. Kusi 2020
amkusinovels@gmail.com
Visit our website at www.amkusi.com
Editor: Anna Bishop of CREATING ink
Sensitivity Edit: Renita McKinney of A Book A Day
Proofreader: Judy's Proofreading
Cover Design: Regina Wamba of ReginaWamba.com
Formatting: Archangel Ink

ISBN: 978-1-949781-16-8

Sign Up to Get New Releases

The best way to get updates about new releases, giveaways, and more is by joining our newsletter. You will also receive a FREE novella to enjoy.

Visit the website below to join:
www.amkusi.com/newsletter

Other Books by A. M. Kusi

A Fallen Star
(Book 1 in The Shattered Cove Series)

Defying Gravity
(Book 3 in The Shattered Cove Series)

The Orchard Inn
(Book 1 in The Orchard Inn Romance Series)

Conflict of Interest
(Book 2 in The Orchard Inn Romance Series)

Her Perfect Storm
(Book 3 in The Orchard Inn Romance Series)

For a complete list of all our books, visit:
www.amkusi.com/books

"Grief never ends, but it changes. It's a passage, not a place to stay. Grief is not a sign of weakness, nor a lack of faith. It is the price of love."

- Unknown

"Trauma compromises our ability to engage with others by replacing patterns of connection with patterns of protection."

- Stephen Porges

Contents

Prologue

Andre
Nine months ago

Andre's soaking wet Henley clung to his skin. His flesh prickled with goose bumps as he made his way home. It had been a long day. He glanced at the clock and winced. *Late.* He pressed his foot a little harder on the gas pedal and shivered. After cranking up the heat, he tapped impatiently on the wheel as a school bus pulled in front of him. He sighed. *This day just keeps getting better.* All Andre wanted was a hot shower and to see his girlfriend's smile. Tiffany should be back from her business trip by now.

As he parked his truck into the driveway, sure enough, there was her car. Large boxes and suitcases were stuffed inside— red flag number one. The weight on his shoulders grew even heavier. *Here we go again.* What could he have done this time? He hadn't seen her in a week because of her job, but he'd made sure to text or try to call her every day like she wanted—even though she'd rarely answered.

Andre got out of the truck and ran through the rain as it pelted against him. He was quick to enter the house and close the door, shielding himself from the elements of the fall rainstorm before he unlaced his work boots.

"Baby?" he called, hesitantly.

"In here," Tiffany answered from the kitchen.

He finished stacking his boots neatly in the entryway and walked in to greet her. She was perched on a barstool, a box of tissues in her hand—red flag number two. He needed a hot shower to soothe his frozen, aching muscles before dealing with one of her famous meltdowns.

His friends had never understood why he stayed with her through their rocky five-year relationship. The heart wants what the heart wants. He tried to hold on to the good memories, the reason he'd fallen head over heels for Tiff as he approached her cautiously.

She sat downcast at the breakfast bar in their kitchen, looking like someone had just killed her puppy. She flicked her eyes up to his before focusing back to her perfectly manicured hands. He'd have to comfort her before he could get into the shower, putting his needs aside to take care of her. *Again.*

"What's wrong?"

"I'm . . . I'm pregnant," she said, sniffling.

He stood frozen as a wave of mixed emotions washed over him—fear, confusion, and excitement. He hadn't planned on having a kid this early in his life, but it could very well be the best thing that ever happened to him. Maybe this could help fix their relationship. Things had been rough, but she was the same girl he'd fallen in love with—and a baby? That was a miracle. Look at his little sister and Lyra. Remy had been a single mother for the first five years of Lyra's life before his brother-in-law pulled his head out of his ass.

He ran a hand over his wet head. "That's great. I mean . . . a baby? Wow. How? We've been so careful."

She swallowed, looking at the counter. Shit. He'd already gone and messed this up.

"I'm not blaming you, babe. It's just so unexpected. This is great!" He put his hand on her belly and she flinched, shaking her head.

"What's wrong?"

"Dre, it's not yours."

It's. Not. Yours.

The words echoed in his mind. The air sucked from his lungs. Unable to draw breath, he clutched his chest. Surely this was a joke. Tiffany was *the one*. Sure, they had their fair share of ups and downs, but didn't every relationship?

"What do you mean?" he asked as he held on to the counter to steady his trembling legs.

"I'm sorry. I didn't mean for you to find out this way." Tears streamed down her face as she reached out to him.

He backed away. "Find out that you've been cheating on me? How long?"

She looked away again.

"How long!" he shouted.

"A year." Her voice was just above a whisper.

She'd been seeing someone for over a year and he'd had no idea. She'd been lying to him. *How could I be so stupid?* She'd made a fool of him.

"All those business trips," he said aloud, everything clicking into place. The shock of it all morphed into rising anger. She'd betrayed him.

"Dre—"

He held up his hand. "Just leave, Tiffany."

"Baby, I'm so sorry. I didn't mean for this to happen. I was sick of being here without anyone giving me attention."

"Don't you dare fucking blame this on me," he roared. "You made a series of choices, and then you fucked another man behind my back and lied to me *for a year*. Get out of my house and don't come back."

She nodded before placing his key on the counter.

Water dripped from his soaked clothes, pooling where he stood like a statue, stone cold, as his whole world crumbled beneath him. Her heels clicked on the tiles as she walked out of his life for good. He braced himself for the slam of the door, but it never came. Hollow silence filled his home. Tears burned his eyes as he swallowed the lump of grief. He wouldn't waste any more time or energy on her.

Andre stalked to his bathroom, stripping off his clothes before he entered the hot spray of the shower. His heart was fractured, breaking apart. How could he have not known? Flashes of all the times she'd been on her phone and full of smiles or taking calls out of earshot of him came back with a vengeance. He had never even thought to check her phone. *Because I believed in her.* He'd given her his trust and his loyalty and where had that gotten him?

He'd been made the fool again. His high-school girlfriend, Teresa, had screwed half the football team before he'd found out. He'd thought that had been a one-off. Apparently not.

Anger radiated through him. He was done with women. He was done with liars. He was just done giving a fuck about anyone but his family and friends. It was safer for his heart that way. He'd never be taken advantage of and played for a fool again.

Chapter 1

Mia

The thud of her shoes hitting the pavement became hypnotic as Mia worked hard to control her breathing. Birds chirped, and the mist began to clear. The rising sun coated her surroundings in an orange glow. This was the best time of day—when everything was mostly quiet, and she could push her body and expel her fears through her sweat.

Her shoulders ached as she pumped her arms a little harder, a little faster. Perhaps she shouldn't have unpacked all those boxes yesterday. But there was no one else to help her do it. After the movers kindly placed her furniture where she needed it, she'd gotten straight to work unpacking. Busyness helped to keep her from thinking too much. *Because thinking leads to remembering.*

Her legs burned as she rounded the corner onto the street where she now lived. Heavy footfalls echoed behind her.

Dios mío. She was alert, as always—every muscle aware that someone was approaching fast from behind. She turned her face quickly, catching a glimpse of a man getting closer. Her shoulders dropped, tension fading. She recognized him. How could she not? He was at least six feet, and muscled to perfection. She'd watched as he exited his truck all sexy and focused the night before. He'd pulled off his shirt, his dark skin glinting from the sun and sweat.

Her handsome new neighbor spoke. "Passing on your right."

"Good morning." She smiled, but he only increased his speed and sprinted ahead of her. Maybe he hadn't heard her? He had earbuds in. Oh well, at least now she had a better view of that tight backside.

Mia pushed herself the remaining several hundred yards to her new home, then trudged up the stairs and into the house, forcing her lead limbs. She grabbed a glass and pushed it into the door of the fridge dispenser. The icy liquid eased down her throat, cooling her body from the inside out. Her muscles were tired, but endorphins were taking over as she gulped fresh oxygen. Time to stretch.

She picked a yoga mat from one of the packing boxes, and opened the French doors leading to the backyard. Whoever had lived here before had kept the landscaping simple. A few flower bushes and trees created a natural line around the bungalow property. A large rectangular pool was the focal point. Maybe she'd go for a swim after her yoga.

Mia started with some simple moves, bending to her knees as she reached her hands out, and stretching her back in extended puppy pose. Breathing deeply, she inhaled light and exhaled her worries. She was intentional, planning her day, giving herself goals and a to-do list.

As she glided through her poses, the hair on the back of her neck stood up. She was being watched. After one more sun salutation, she glanced around, catching a glimpse of *him* on the second-floor balcony of his house.

His lips flattened and his brow furrowed. He seemed

downright angry and snarling. A flurry of confused butterflies swirled in her belly. She waved, breaking their awkward staring contest, hoping her smile would set him at ease.

He turned quickly, entering his house, seemingly ignoring her. Well, okay then. Who pissed in his cornflakes? *"Sometimes it's the people who deserve kindness the least who need it the most."* Her mother's words echoed in her mind. Maybe she should properly introduce herself. Her mamá's recipe for polvorones was irresistible, and something told her she could use the sweet gift as the perfect icebreaker for her grumpy new neighbor.

* * *

After a shower and a quick change into some cutoffs and a faded T-shirt, she pulled her dark brown hair into a ponytail. First on her agenda was coffee, and then groceries.

As she drove along the road of the quiet neighborhood, a feeling of calm settled over her. Kids were laughing and throwing Frisbees or playing catch with their dogs. The houses were all well-kept and lawns neatly manicured. How long had she wished she could live in a place like this? Too bad her mother wasn't there to see she'd actually made it happen.

Mia switched on the radio. A few of the latest hits blasted out as she headed towards town. The woods on her right opened up, and the beautiful coastline was breathtaking. Green-blue waves crashed onto the rocky shore. Mia rolled down the window, inhaling the salty air. The urge to pull over and dip her toes in the cool water was overwhelming. She slowed as she rounded the corner. A blue car was parked at the edge of the road with smoke billowing out of the propped-open hood. A woman with black hair held a baby and was staring off towards the waves.

Mia pulled behind the car and parked before getting out. "Are you alright?"

The woman turned, wiping away fresh tears as her cheeks blushed. "Oh, sorry. Uh . . ." The baby she held started to cry. Her mother shifted to bounce and rock the child.

"Are you alright?" Mia repeated, stepping closer.

"No. I'm sorry. I'm not usually a crier. It's just been a really tough . . . year," she said as if she was trying to remember a time when life wasn't hard. Mia could relate. The baby drifted off to sleep, seemingly calmed by her mother's voice.

"We all have bad days. Can I help? I can give you a ride. I was just on my way into town anyways," Mia offered.

A spark of hope lit the woman's almond-shaped eyes. "Would you mind? I don't want to sit around waiting for my brother to find a tow. You can drop me off at my sister-in-law's café. It's right on Main Street."

"Absolutely. I needed some coffee anyways. I'm Mia." She reached out her hand.

"Jasmine, and this is Zoey." The woman shook her hand.

"She's beautiful. How old?" Mia asked as they walked towards their vehicles.

"Almost seven months."

Mia helped secure the car seat, following Jasmine's detailed directions. After Jasmine laid the sleeping baby down and buckled her in, they headed towards town.

"Do you live around here?" Jasmine tucked a black tendril of hair behind her ear.

"Yes, just moved in yesterday."

"Oh, where are you from?"

"California. I needed a change of pace but I wanted to be by the ocean, so New Hampshire it was." Mia gave her the carefully practiced answer that stayed as close to the truth as possible while omitting the important details.

"That's a long way from home. What do you do for work?" Jasmine asked.

"I'm opening a yoga studio."

"Yoga? Sounds interesting, but I don't think it's really my thing."

"Well, when the studio opens, you'll have to come check it out. I'd be happy to teach you. I'd love to have company in the meantime. Free sessions until the studio opens. It's a great way to ground yourself. It's helped me deal with stressful life moments." She hoped she wasn't giving too much of herself away, but this was the reason she taught yoga in the first place.

Jasmine seemed thoughtful. "Maybe."

Mia smiled. She felt a pull towards this woman for some reason. Maybe she and Jasmine had something in common.

"Do you have any family in the area?" Jasmine asked.

"No. It's uh . . . just me."

"Mine are gone too," Jasmine said as their gazes met.

"You said you had a brother?" Mia asked, turning onto Main Street.

Jasmine nodded. "Yeah, two actually. Mikel is married to Remy. She owns the Stardust Café—right here on the left. You can park anywhere. And Bently is the oldest."

Mia did as she directed.

"What about you? Any siblings?" Jasmine asked, unbuckling herself and gathering the diaper bag.

"Nope. Just me."

"I don't know what I'd do without my brothers. Especially

Bently, the oldest. He basically raised me, and then he jumped in to help me when I found out I was pregnant."

"Oh. Zoey's dad isn't in the picture?" Mia asked.

Jasmine hesitated and drew in a breath. "No."

There was a story there. Mia reached out her hand instinctively to comfort her. "I was raised by a single mom, and though I always missed my dad, she gave me enough love for the both of them." Mia smiled, trying to lighten the mood. "I liked hearing about you and your family. I'd be happy to be a listening ear if you ever need to talk."

"Let's exchange numbers." Jasmine offered, pulling out her phone.

Mia helped Jasmine carry the car seat into the Stardust Café. The smell of fresh coffee and sugary treats instantly enveloped her. A sign in bold lettering made it clear that all of the offerings were gluten-free. She hoped they didn't taste it.

"Hey, Jasmine. What happened?" a beautiful woman in a flowery sundress asked from behind the counter.

Jasmine nodded for Mia to follow her through the back to the kitchen.

"Long story. Mia here was kind enough to be my heroine. Mia, this is Remy, my sister-in-law."

Remy took baby Zoey from Jasmine and gave her cheek a kiss before she reached out to shake Mia's hand. Mia set the car seat on the floor.

"Mia, it's nice to meet you. Are you new in town?" Remy asked as Zoey wrapped her chubby fist around and pulled one of her braids.

"Yes, I just moved from California."

"Wow. That's quite the change of pace, I'm sure. You

couldn't have picked a better town. What do you do for work?" Remy asked.

"She's not going to work at your café, Rem. She's a business owner herself," Jasmine interjected, taking a cookie off the cooling rack.

"Oh, you are? What kind of business?" Remy asked, adjusting Zoey on her other hip.

"I'm opening a yoga studio."

"Good. We need more women in business in this town." Remy smiled.

"Are there many?" Mia asked.

"Besides my café, and Jasmine's bed-and-breakfast, there's the book store, but I can't think of any other businesses owned solely by a woman."

"You own a bed-and-breakfast?" Mia asked Jasmine.

"Yes, The Lighthouse Inn. About two miles down the coast from where you found me stranded." Jasmine turned to Remy. "Doesn't Charli own the bar?"

Remy shook her head. "No, her husband's parents still do, but she basically runs the whole place. I never see Zeke or Claire there anymore."

Jasmine nodded.

Zoey reached for the remaining cookie in her mother's hand.

"She's just like her mommy—a sugar addict." Remy smiled.

"Let's hope that's all she gets from me," Jasmine said, seemingly hiding behind a smile as she handed over a large cookie crumb to her daughter.

Remy's expression morphed into concern. "You're doing

an amazing job. She's loved and fed and clothed. What more could a baby want?"

"Mia needs some caffeine," Jasmine said, quickly changing the subject, taking Zoey back in her arms.

"What can I get you?" Remy asked.

"Just a black coffee, with one of your lavender scones," Mia answered.

"Coming right up." Remy walked back out into the main part of the café and started making the coffee.

Jasmine spoke. "I just wanted to thank you again for helping me out today and letting me vent. I'd really love to pay you back in some way. I'm having a barbecue at The Lighthouse Inn this evening. Remy will be there, and my brothers—just a few friends and fellow local business owners getting together to have a drink and some great food. Remy is making dinner. I'd love if you came as my guest."

Mia smiled as her chest tightened. She liked Jasmine, and the woman seemed genuine and friendly. She could use a friend right now—hers were thousands of miles away on the other side of the country.

You have to put yourself out there.

"Sure. That sounds fun. Let me know if I can bring anything."

Remy came back into the kitchen, handing her the coffee and a wax paper bag. Mia wrapped her fingers around the warm paper cup, breathing in the delicious aroma. "Thank you. How much do I owe you?"

Remy shook her head, her braids swaying with the motion. "It's on the house."

"I appreciate it."

"Do you have any family out here?" Remy asked.

Mia sipped the coffee before shaking her head. "No. My mother died last year and my father passed when I was a child."

"Oh, I'm sorry," Remy said.

Mia gave her a polite smile.

"I really hope you'll come tonight," Jasmine said.

Remy glanced at her sister-in-law. "Oh, yes! Please come. I'd love to hear more about your plans for the studio."

"I'll text you the address," Jasmine added.

"Alright. Sure." Mia agreed before saying goodbye and thanking Remy one more time for the coffee. She got into her car and took a bite of the lavender scone. An explosion of flavor filled her mouth. The floral essence of lavender mixed with the flaky sweetness of the scone. Seemed like the gluten-free pastries might just be better than she'd thought, much like the locals in this new town. She smiled and headed towards the grocery store.

* * *

Hours later, Mia placed the last polvorones on the plate and licked her finger clean of the powdered sugar. They were still warm—just the way she liked them. She slipped on a pair of flip-flops and walked over to her neighbor's door and knocked. She waited patiently, nerves filling her belly as she carefully balanced the plate of cookies in her hands. It was important to have a good relationship with your new neighbors—and food was the way to everyone's heart.

The pounding of footsteps came closer. A dark shadow passed behind the thick glass of the door just before it flew open. Her neighbor's confused expression quickly morphed into one of anger.

What the fuck is his problem?

"H-hi. I'm Mia, your new neighbor. I thought I'd introduce myself."

He towered over her, jaw clenched. His hands fisted at his sides as his eyes raked over her body. She was sure that was lust in his dark gaze, but the man also seemed livid just with her presence.

"I brought you some polvorones. You might have heard them called Mexican wedding cookies here."

He stared at the plate, his jaw ticcing. More awkward silence.

"Um . . . did I do something to upset you?" she asked, her patience wearing thin.

Something hesitant flashed in his eyes, but then it was gone. "Stay the fuck away from me," he growled just before slamming the door in her face.

She was too stunned to speak. What a complete asshole. The nerve of this guy. She'd tried to be friendly. No one turned down her mother's recipe.

Oh well, at least now she'd have something to bring to the barbecue. She needed a reminder that there were some people in this town who were decent human beings.

One thing was for sure—her neighbor wasn't one of them. And she'd be damned if she ever tried to be nice to him again. She'd just have to avoid him like the plague, neighbor or not.

Chapter 2

Andre

Pulling on a clean T-shirt, Andre ran through the to-do list in his mind, checking off all that he had accomplished for the day. His team had completed a contract on a renovation that afternoon.

Seaview Construction was so close to hitting the goals he and Mikel had set when they'd first started the business as a side gig years ago. With Mikel back, things were finally starting to move in the right direction.

He righted his pants and fastened a black belt around his waist. A flash of something white caught his eye. The new neighbor's bedroom was directly across from his. She was sitting, only visible from the lap up. She seemed to be on the phone and laughing about something. His cock stirred to life. His body tensed in anger.

Women were all the same. They were all Tiffanys and Teresas. So why was it this one had made him feel something, this desire to take a fistful of that ponytail he'd seen jogging in front of him and pound into her from behind?

Hormones. Nothing more, nothing less. Or maybe she was a witch. Either way, it didn't matter. All that mattered was that she stayed out of his life—which he hoped he'd made clear during her visit earlier. It wasn't like him to be so rude to a woman, but something came over him every time he looked at her. That something was the reason he needed to stay far away from her.

Fuck, I don't need this right now.

Maybe he should take Bently's advice and try one-night stands occasionally. All that built-up sexual tension was what this was. As much as his cock wanted to, he would not explore that option with his neighbor.

Andre's phone rang. *Mikel.*

"Hey, what's up?"

"I just wanted to tell you I met with a new client today and got the paperwork finalized. She's paying extra to have us start the renovation on Monday. You good to go?"

"Yeah, we finished the Vaughn job this afternoon. I did the final walk-through with him. What is it this time?"

"A studio reno. It's gutted already, starting mostly from scratch," Mikel answered.

"Sure, I'll stop in the office Monday and get the paperwork, then we can head to the site to meet the client."

"Sounds like a plan. This job is gonna be big, bro. This is the one that puts us ahead of projection," Mikel said.

"Well then, I better not fuck it up." Andre chuckled.

"Yeah. I'll see you soon." Mikel laughed.

"Yup."

Andre ended the call before throwing the phone onto the bed. He peeked outside the window, the white billowing curtains moving aside to show her floral comforter, now devoid of the bewitching woman with the coffee hair. Why did that disappoint him?

He grabbed a snap-back hat from his closet before heading towards his car.

* * *

As he carried the case of IPA around the back of Jasmine's bed-and-breakfast, the familiar sound of his friends' laughter against the steady crashing of waves on the beach filled him with joy. This was what he wanted in life—to succeed with his business, and to share good times with his friends and family.

"Oh my God! What a jerk," Remy said as he rounded the corner.

Whoa. He was for sure seeing things. Could a lack of sex cause you to hallucinate? Sitting next to his sister and Jasmine at the very picnic table he'd shared countless meals and laughs with his friends was the unmistakable sexy body of his new neighbor.

Fuck me.

"Who's a jerk?" Andre's voice boomed, louder than he'd intended.

All eyes turned to gaze at him. Mia's mouth parted as surprise painted her features. She seemed just as shocked to see him. *What is she doing here?*

"Dre, you have to hear what an absolute a-s-s-h-o-l-e Mia's neighbor is," Remy answered, spelling out the curse as his niece Lyra ran in a circle around the table of adults.

I'm an asshole? Hot anger boiled his blood. His body tensed, burning with unchecked rage. Why was she here? This was his sacred place with *his* friends. She was sitting in his goddamn seat.

Mia blinked a few times, neither one of them speaking.

"Uncle Dre!" Lyra ran up to him, breaking the staring contest.

"Hey, princess. You've grown since I last saw you." Andre focused his attention on his niece. She was the perfect mix of Mikel and Remy with light-brown skin and curly dark hair.

"Phoenix grew too. Come see my baby brother." Lyra held his hand with hers and led him towards the table where Bently reached out and grabbed the case from him.

"Oh, good, you brought my favorite," Bently said, quickly popping off a tab.

Is Mia here with Bently? The thought brought a scorching sensation to his chest. *Heartburn.*

"Dre, meet Mia. She just moved to town," Jasmine said.

"How did you all meet?" he asked, his gaze on Mia, who was holding baby Zoey. God, why did that sight tear him apart and seem to put him back together all at once? This was *his* family. Why was she here invading *his* space?

"Mia saved me. My car broke down and she gave Zoey and me a ride to Remy's," Jasmine explained.

"You got in a car with a stranger?" Dre asked, concerned.

"Not all people are jerks," Mia said, as if she was defending Jasmine.

"I'd have gotten in the car with you too." Bently smiled and gave Mia a wink.

Andre's stomach roiled. The little witch had put all his friends under her spell.

"Back to this neighbor. What exactly happened?" Andre asked, seeing how far he could push her.

Mia swallowed and straightened her spine before she looked him in the eye and answered, "He ignored me when I said good morning, but I chalked that up to the fact that he

18

probably didn't hear me with his earbuds in. Then I waved hello, and he downright scowled at me. I figured I would give him one more chance—maybe he was having a bad day. I baked cookies." She nodded towards the pile of desserts covered in powdered sugar on the table in front of them as Bently reached for one. "Strike three. He shut the door in my face."

"Maybe he didn't want to be bothered," Andre said, leaning in.

"Or maybe he's just an a-s-s-h-o-l-e," she said almost as if it was a challenge.

"Only an idiot would turn down your cookies, Mia," Bently said, smirking.

Andre clenched his fists. Were his friends taking her side? They hadn't even been there. Women were all the same. Mia was a fake and a temptress.

"I agree." She smiled, and good God—how could he hate something and love it all at once?

"Who is this guy? I'll pay him a visit. Sounds like he needs to learn a few manners. What's his address?" Bently asked.

"Autumn Street," Mia answered.

Bently hesitated a moment and then looked at Andre. "You live on that street. Any idea who she's talking about?"

"Nope." He played dumb, part of him wanting to see how she would react.

"Really?" Mia challenged.

"What's wrong if a man doesn't want to say hello, or wave back, or have his day disturbed by a perky stranger with cookies? Who knows what you could have put in them," Andre defended, his voice rising in anger. He grabbed a bottle of beer and twisted the cap off before gulping down half the bottle.

"Dude, chill out," Bently said, eyeing him warily.

"Are you her neighbor?" Remy asked.

His friends' shocked and intense gazes were all aimed at him. They'd been turned against him after one meeting with this woman.

Mia bit her bottom lip, seeming unsure. *Now she wants to be quiet.*

Remy handed baby Phoenix to Bently before she stood. "Dre, can I talk to you for a second?"

"Fine," he said, following after her while draining the last of his beer. They walked towards the beach, out of earshot of the rest of their friends.

"What is going on with you?" Remy asked, getting straight to the point.

"Nothing."

"Don't give me that crap answer. You're being mean to that woman. She's a guest and a new friend of Jasmine's and mine. Why would you be so rude to a person who came to introduce herself to you? This isn't like you, Dre." Remy worried her brow.

"Don't you see? She's playing you all."

"What I see is the anger you have for what Tiffany did to you. That was a year ago. You need to move on and stop assuming all other women you meet are like her," Remy said.

"I'm fine, Remy. I'm over Tiffany." It still hurt to say her name.

"Mia seems like a good person. Jasmine was having a tough day and Mia helped make it better. She has no one else. No family or friends here, and you aren't giving her a very good impression of Shattered Cove."

She was alone? "Fine."

"What is that supposed to mean?"

Andre sighed. "It means I'll be cordial to her. Happy?"

Remy shook her head. "It's a start."

Andre put his arm around his sister as they walked back to their friends. Mia was nowhere in sight. Had she left? Did he care? He walked into the bed-and-breakfast through the screen door, past the kitchen, and found the bathroom door closed, so he knocked.

"I'll be right out," Mia's voice said from within. She sniffled.

Had he made her cry? A pang of guilt shot through his chest, unsettling him. Why should he care about this woman's feelings? It was probably just an act for sympathy. Tiffany used to cry too. But his ex had never done it privately—it was always out in the open to manipulate him. So, maybe Mia was sincere? He should just bite the bullet and apologize.

She opened the door, chocolate tresses spilling around her face. The scent of spicy roses enveloped him. The flash of vulnerability in her eyes made something deep and primal surge inside him. Up close, her beauty shocked his system with white-hot lust. His body reacted before his mind could catch up. Andre stepped into her space, crowding her against the door as his body towered over hers. Those big chocolate eyes staring up at him burned with fire.

"W-what are you doing?" she asked, her voice holding only a slight tremor.

"I have no fucking clue." *But I can't stop it. And that makes it all the worse.*

Her chest rose and fell. Her breasts pressed against his chest as they stared at each other in silence for a few seconds.

She stood taller. "I would appreciate some personal space."

"Liar," he said. It was clear from the way her eyes dilated and her breathing shallowed she was just as attracted to him as he was to her. "I fucking hate liars."

"I hate assholes who think they can be mean and expect women to fall at their feet. Let's be clear, Andre, was it? The only one falling to their knees will be you," Mia said.

He was so distracted by her feistiness, instantly addicted to the challenge between them, that he didn't understand why he was suddenly, in fact, on his knees holding his junk as it radiated with pain. He groaned and hissed through his gritted teeth. *She kneed me in the balls!*

Leaning down, she said, "Next time a woman tells you to give them space, you better listen." She stepped over him and walked out.

Damn! He hadn't seen that coming.

After a few minutes, Andre composed himself. Shit. He had been a dick. He wasn't acting like himself whenever she was around. His mother would kill him if she found out about the way he'd treated Mia. Whatever. It wasn't like he was going to have to see her again. He could avoid her easily enough at home, go jogging earlier, and close his blinds on her side of the property. If Jasmine and Remy hung out with her, he'd avoid that too.

Andre walked to the backyard. Mikel had finally arrived.

"Hey, Dre. Small world, isn't it?" Mikel asked.

"How so?" Andre asked.

Mikel smiled. "Mia Garcia is the owner of the yoga studio we start renovations on next."

Chapter 3

Mia

The next morning, Mia's legs ached as she turned onto her road. The birdsong and the rustle of the trees were her background music as she jogged towards her home. The heavy footfalls from behind her got closer. The hair on the back of her neck stood to attention. Her belly flipped and twisted into knots.

Was it him? Andre Stone was the only one who'd ever had her so tied up. Finding out her new friends were connected to him had stolen the breath from her lungs. Having him corner her in that bathroom had thrown her off her axis. He'd called her a liar, and it was like he could see through her. How did he know? Besides, not all lies were bad. *Sometimes lives depend on lies.*

She turned to look over her shoulder. His eyes darted from her backside to the road in front of them. Apparently, he wasn't so immune either. Andre increased his speed yet again and passed her, his manly scent drifting over to tease her senses. Her already sweaty body had now gone up an extra ten degrees instantaneously. Why did this man affect her so overwhelmingly?

Too bad he had to be an asshole.

* * *

Mia made it back to her house, drinking some cool water before venturing to the backyard to move through her yoga poses. This time she didn't have an audience.

After she showered, she got dressed in a simple pair of dark purple leggings that came to her calf and a black muscle shirt. She checked her watch. She had a few minutes to call Carmen before she headed towards the studio to meet the construction crew.

She pressed her friend's contact information and the call buzzed through.

"Mia! *Amiga, cómo estás?*"

Mia smiled. "*Bien! Y tú?*"

"*Niná,* I miss you so much. I know you said you needed a change, but why did it have to be on the other side of the country?" Carmen asked.

Mia sighed. "I just wanted a fresh start. Too many memories back there."

"Running from your *problemas* won't make them disappear, *cariño,*" Carmen warned.

"I know. But it's been mostly good things over here so far," Mia said.

"Yeah? Have you made some friends? How's the studio coming?" Carmen asked.

Mia smiled. "I did happen to make a couple new acquaintances. One woman owns a café here in town and the other a bed-and-breakfast."

"Oh, good. So we have somewhere to stay when Mamá, Papi, Mateo, and I come to visit."

"Yes. And I am heading out as soon as I get off the phone

with you to meet the guys at the studio to begin renovations," Mia added.

"I'm so excited for you. Mateo has been asking how you are doing," Carmen said.

"I'll call him sometime soon. Give your parents and brother a hug for me."

"I will. *Te amo, chica,*" Carmen said, before making a kiss sound.

"I love you too."

* * *

Thirty minutes later, Mia pulled into the parking lot of her new yoga studio. She stacked the boxes of donuts and placed the several cups of coffee on top, balancing the paper bag full of sugar and creamer as well. She walked towards the door as someone came from behind her to hold the door open.

"Good morning, Mia."

"*Buenos días.*" She smiled back, entering where her future lobby would be. Mikel took the cups of coffee and the paper bag from the top of her pile and placed them on the card table set up in the corner with a few stacks of papers and tools.

"You brought sustenance?" Mikel asked.

"Yes. I figured your team would need it for the long day ahead."

A few men wandered in and out with tape measures and various tools. Nerves somersaulted in her belly. This was it—the first step in making her dreams come true and fulfilling her promise to her mother.

"Dre!" Mikel called.

Oh no. It couldn't be . . . could it?

Andre's dark eyes met hers only momentarily as he entered

the room. He had a tool belt clipped around his waist and tan Carhartt pants that led to his worn work boots. She swallowed, trying not to think that how he looked in a hard hat was a fantasy come to life.

Mikel came to her rescue, focusing her thoughts back to the job at hand. "So, let's do one more walk-through to make sure we're all on the same page before we begin construction. Sound good?"

Mia nodded.

As they went room by room, Mia paid careful attention to the detail that Mikel went into. She'd hired the right crew, even if that meant putting up with her ornery neighbor for the time being.

"I thought we were going to move this wall?" she asked.

Andre shook his head, and then spoke for the first time. "Can't. It's a load-bearing wall."

"But I need this space opened up to have it feel airy," she argued.

"No can do." Andre smirked.

Anger lit her skin on fire at the same time as his smile brought heat to another part of her traitorous body.

"I think we've come up with a solution you might be happy with. Andre suggested we turn this wall over here," Mikel said, pointing, "into a giant window. That would make this space feel more open while not causing structural issues."

"Andre had this idea, huh?" she asked as she studied the broody six-foot man.

"Couldn't let a project be done half-baked since it has my name on it," Andre said as if insinuating somehow the shortcoming would be her fault.

This man liked to stir up trouble where there was none. He got under her skin like no one ever had.

"I wouldn't expect anything less from someone *I* hired," she said, letting him know exactly who was in charge here.

Mikel stepped in front of his business partner and guided her along. She caught the death glare he gave Andre as they passed.

"Now, let's talk about this flooring. It's really nice hardwood. It almost feels sacrilegious to pull it up. Are you sure you want to do that?" Mikel asked. "It would save you a few thousand to leave it be."

His phone rang, interrupting her response.

"Sorry. It's my wife. I should take this. She doesn't call unless it's important," Mikel explained.

"Go ahead." She nodded.

"Why are we ripping up hardwood floors? They're timeless, durable, and eco-friendly. We can sand and stain them a different color if that's the reason," Andre said, stepping closer into her space. You'd have thought he'd have learned his lesson last time.

"You really don't think I know anything, do you? I'm having a shipment of selenite crystals delivered to the studio. I want the bags of crushed stones to be distributed underneath. Then you can relay the flooring." She wouldn't tell him that it was because it was her only connection to her mother. That she wanted a piece of Mamá to always be in the foundation of making her dream come true.

His mouth hung open as he stared at her speechless. "Rocks? You want to throw away thousands of dollars and a ton of man hours to rip up a floor and put rocks in it?" He burst out laughing. The harder he laughed, the angrier she got.

He had no idea what this place meant to her. What it was like to have nothing left of your parents, to live through the tragedy she had. She clenched her fists. *"El Cabrón!"*

"You're crazy, woman!" He held his stomach as another fit of laughter overtook him.

"That is something people say when they don't understand something. When it's too big for them to wrap their little minds around. You work for me. I didn't hire you to see my vision. I hired you to bring it to life."

He stood taller, finally getting a hold of himself before he shrugged. "Your money to waste." Her victory was short-lived as his eyes narrowed in on her. "Unless it's Mommy and Daddy's dollar and you're just some rich spoiled princess with no idea what she's doing."

It was the furthest thing from the truth.

The blood drained from her face as she blinked. The heavy weight settling on her chest made it hard to breathe. *No, not here. Not in front of him.* She searched around them for her quickest escape route. She would not have a panic attack in here. She turned away as the tears stung her eyes. She swallowed the lump of emotion that roiled within her. She counted, trying to slow her inhales, as his strong hand wrapped around her arm, pulling her back to face him.

"Running away from the tru—" Andre stopped. His anger morphed into a flash of something softer before letting her go.

She spun back to the exit and forced her legs not to run out of the room, hoping to hold on to a shred of dignity. Mia left embarrassed, determined to never let herself be so vulnerable with that man again.

28

Chapter 4

Andre

Friday morning came around more slowly than Andre had ever thought possible. After his argument with Mia, he'd felt like an ass. He'd recognized the panicked expression in her eyes—it was the same one his friend Bently would get whenever his past threatened to catch up with him.

The rest of the week Andre kept to himself, working alongside his team to put up Sheetrock and open the wall they'd agreed to add several glass plates to, converting it into a giant window. He'd plugged in earbuds and focused on the tasks at hand, ignoring her curvy ass in skintight yoga pants or shorts, depending on the day. He'd always been one to admire a nice booty, but Mia's was downright perfection. His team had seemed to notice as well. He'd barked at more than one of his guys to stay professional on the job.

On Tuesday, Mia had eaten lunch with the crew. They'd all sat on whatever they could find, but when Mia came over, they all jumped to their feet to offer her their makeshift chairs. Wednesday, he'd had to snap at them more than once to get back to work rather than chat it up with her. By Thursday, he'd about given up. If he heard her laugh at something Stan or Tom said one more time, or ask about their kids by name, he'd fucking lose it.

He went to bed hard as a rock every single night. He hated her for what she did to him. He hated her warm smile, and her throaty laughter, and the way she rolled her R's, and how cute her accent was. It was like the woman was designed for the single purpose of making him crave her. Mia was the ultimate test of his self-control. She was feisty, and not afraid of confrontation—his sore groin was proof of that. And lately, he'd seen a softer side to her in the way she interacted with people.

He slammed the car door and walked back to the work site after his trip to the bank. Thank goodness she hadn't been in today. He wasn't sure how much more of her he could take. He walked past the team, glancing at the wrapped sub in one of his worker's hands. "Treating yourself, Stan?"

Stan looked up and smiled. "Mia brought it in for me. She got pizza for Tom. And even bought us some cookies from the café to bring home to our families." Stan's blue eyes sparkled as he nodded towards the back room.

She was here? *Damn it.* So much for a reprieve. And how did she know their favorites? She'd won over his crew with bribery—*little witch*—cast them all under her spell. She even had Mikel on her side.

Andre nodded and walked towards the hall where Mikel was studying an invoice.

"Remind me again why we can't get out of this contract," Andre groaned.

Mikel gave him an incredulous look. "You know why. It's bad for business to back out, especially after we already started the work. This is a huge job that helps us achieve our goals for the year. Not to mention, my wife would kill me if we didn't complete it."

"Why is Remy suddenly so invested in this?" Andre asked, bewildered.

Mikel shook his head. "Your sister likes Mia. They're becoming friends, and she thinks Mia will be good for you."

"What? Why?" Andre grimaced.

"You really don't see? Man, Tiff did a number on you."

Andre's muscles tensed with anger at the mention of his ex. "Why does everyone keep bringing her up? I'm over her."

Mikel gave him a knowing look. "You keep telling yourself that. I know firsthand how that anger festers inside you. You think it's safer to keep everyone out, but what you're really doing is punishing yourself. Tiffany's off living her life and you're here alone and angry. Tell me again how much you're over her."

Andre clenched his fists. His friend spoke the truth, but it didn't mean he was ready to hear it. "I'm not lonely. I have a business and my friends and family. That's all I need."

"Whatever you say," Mikel said, holding up both hands as if to calm a wild beast.

The scent of something herbal caught his attention. Andre sniffed. *What is that . . .? Is it . . .*

"Who the hell is smoking weed?" Andre darted out of the room, following the scent to where it grew stronger. All his men seemed to be accounted for, working. That only left one possibility. He opened the door to what would be the office, and sure enough, Mia stood there with a lighter in one hand and a long bundle of green in another. "What the fuck are you doing? Smoking weed while we're trying to work?"

Mia whipped around. *"Dios mío!"* She clutched her chest,

her surprise quickly morphing into fury. "Does this look like marijuana to you?" She held out the bundle of dried herbs, still billowing smoke from one end.

"Well, what the hell is it?" he barked.

"It's sage. I'm using sage to clear this space of negative energy. If I'd have known you'd be here, I would have brought more—maybe just built a bonfire under you and lit the whole place on fire."

His mind was reeling. The way she furrowed her brow and argued with him was like foreplay. Being around her was like being in a constant state of torture. She was drugging him—that was it. This little witch was using magic on him. "Your voodoo won't work on me." He smirked.

She rolled her eyes. God damnit, even her disrespect was cute.

"You think I don't see what you're doing here?" he growled.

She placed the burning sage into an empty cup on the desk and the lighter in her pocket before crossing her arms, drawing his attention to her perfect breasts.

She replied, her voice sounding innocent, "Why don't you enlighten me—seeing how you think you are so much smarter than me. Oh, high and mighty one, please tell this . . . rich princess, was it? Tell me what my secret evil plans are."

His cock stirred as she stood taller, challenging him. He stepped closer. The triangle in her forehead deepened.

"You have every man in this place wrapped around your finger. Somehow, you even have my sister and best friend on your side. But I know something they don't, little witch."

She moved further into his person space, her spicy rose scent mixing with the sage. She was intoxicating. He swayed on his feet as she spoke. "And what is that?" Her voice was breathy, waking parts of him that he didn't want to feel.

"You're a liar. A fake."

She blinked, an emotion he couldn't name flashing in her eyes before she narrowed her gaze on him. A sly smile crept across her features as she looked him up and down. She leaned in, her mouth only a breath away from his. His entire body was burning in an inferno with her closeness. Andre's self-control threatened to snap.

She whispered, "Andre Stone, I see you. You have the eyes of a man who once felt passion in his life. But that fire has gone out now. Someone hurt you, *deeply*. You built walls around your heart, and your brain sends shit like that out of your mouth as a defense mechanism."

His brow furrowed and he shook his head. "A defense against what?"

"I think what you see as a lie is my ability to believe in something greater than myself. Something you've lost."

His ears were ringing, blood flowing fast. She was right—to deny it would make him the liar.

"Your friends seem to think you're a good guy, and yet you're a jerk to me." She looked him in the eye and continued, "It makes me wonder if it's me, or if every woman is your target simply because of our sex."

Oh, God. That three-letter word falling from her full lips made a scorching fireball of lust combust inside him. What was she saying? All he could focus on were those lips he wanted to bite—her seductive voice he wanted to hear scream his name. Even the way she argued was erotic.

He reached out and grabbed her shoulders, anger rising, mixed with lust. She gasped, and the zing of his skin against hers sent electricity radiating through him. *What the hell?* He was drawn to her with a magnanimity that he'd never felt before, and that was enough of a warning. She brought out a side to him that had never seen the light of day. This Andre was animalistic in the way he craved her. "I don't hate women. Just you."

She smiled and it was like gasoline on the fire raging inside him. He gripped her more firmly. He wasn't hurting her, only holding her securely away from him. He needed to get his body under control. She had the upper hand and she knew it.

"Is that why you can't keep your hands off me?" She searched his eyes, a small smile playing on the corner of her mouth.

God, he wanted to taste her lips.

"Let me go," she said, her voice breathy.

He dropped his hands to his sides instantly. What was he doing? He ran a palm over his head. This woman made him react in ways he'd never experienced before. He wasn't sure which way was up or down anymore. She knocked him for a loop, and he was spinning uncontrollably, drifting aimlessly in space.

Mia gave him one last look of appraisal before she left the room. Andre tried calming the swell of emotion that rose in his chest: lust and fury. Who would have known it would be so addictive? He needed a few strong drinks and a quick fuck to get his body back in control. He pulled out his phone and texted Bently.

Andre: *Shipwreck later? I need a wingman.*

Bently: *Has hell frozen over?*

Andre: *Don't flatter yourself.*

Bently: *See ya at six.*

Chapter 5

Andre

Andre settled onto a barstool at The Shipwreck.
Charli greeted him. "Hey, handsome. What can I get ya?"

"Jack and Coke, please."

"Coming right up."

As she poured the whiskey into the glass, he asked, "How's that man of yours?"

She was beaming. "He's hanging in there. Only a handful of months on his deployment left."

"That's awesome. Pass on my gratitude," Andre said as she handed him his drink.

"Will do. Should I start a tab?"

"Yeah, that's probably best," Andre answered. He had no intention of stopping at one. He needed to let loose and relax.

"Put a beer on his tab for me too. One of those new Long Trails you got in last week," Bently said, slapping Andre's back.

"Buy your own beer, Sheriff," Andre teased.

"Oh, come on. You invited me. That's no way to treat a guest who's doing you a favor," Bently argued.

"You act as if you'd not have been here if I hadn't texted you. This is your go-to for a Friday night."

Bently shook his head. "Nah, I've been cutting back on my appearances. Haven't I, Charli baby?"

Charli smiled and handed him his draft. "I'll admit I've been seeing less of your face than usual."

"Bet you miss these baby blues, don't ya? When you gonna leave that man of yours and run away with me?" Bently flirted.

Charli shook her head. "You know better than that. No one can compare to my soldier."

Bently sighed. "Ugh, you're breaking my heart. Just give me one night to change your mind."

Charli smiled. "One of these days your charm is gonna get you in trouble, Bently Evans."

"Baby, trouble is my middle name," Bently said.

Andre held up a hand. "Alright, Casanova, leave the woman alone. You're here to help me find a date for tonight."

Bently set his beer on the bar and clapped his hands before rubbing them together. "Alright. Any preference?"

"Just someone for tonight only, and no one we know. She can't be related to anyone we know either." That was just bad for business.

"Geez. You expect a lot from a small-town watering hole. We should have met up in the city. That's where I usually go to find someone I don't know and will never see again." Bently shook his head.

Andre took another sip of his drink, the burn of the alcohol mixing with the bubbles in the soda down his throat.

"Wow. I think I found the exception to your criteria," Bently said, slapping Andre's shoulder.

"Where?" Andre said, searching the room. His eyes zoned in on skinny-jean-clad legs and an off-shoulder black top with the most perfect set of breasts he'd ever seen. The only problem was, he had seen them before.

Mia walked across the room, her long chocolate-colored hair spilling over her shoulders, those wide dark eyes taking in the room.

"Not a chance," Andre growled, focusing back on his drink.

"Are you kidding me? Are you sure you even like women? Maybe you're gay? You'd have to be to not want to bring her home, even if you have to see her again. Maybe it could be a regular casual thing?" Bently offered, his hungry gaze never leaving Mia.

"I think I'd know if I liked dick by now, don't you?" Andre argued.

"Well, if you're sure. You know you'd still be my brother from another mother, right?" Bently said.

"I'm positive I'm not gay."

"Then, I guess I'm gonna go and see if she wants my company," Bently said, grabbing his beer.

Before Andre could react, his friend was gone, approaching Mia. His stomach roiled as he clenched his fists. Why the fuck was he jealous? The thought of his friend's hands all over the lush curves he wanted to explore invaded his mind. Mia shuddering from his touch, screaming Bently's name instead of his.

"God damnit!" Andre slammed his hand on the bar top.

"Hey, everything okay?" Charli asked.

"Just peachy." He couldn't escape Mia. Everywhere he went, she popped up. At home, work, and now during his time with *his* friends. What if Bently dated her? Andre chuckled to himself. Bently didn't date anyone. He was a one-and-done type of guy.

"Charli, give me a whiskey—three fingers."

She eyed him warily. "Coming right up."

Mia's laugh assaulted his ears. He knew if he turned around, he'd see Bently's hands all over her as they danced. Or maybe he was bending her over the pool table showing her exactly how he'd use his stick. Andre ran a hand over his face and let out a frustrated breath. He needed to get this out of his system one way or another.

Charli set the glass in front of him and he chugged down the liquor as it burned his throat. He slammed the empty glass on the bar and turned around, searching for someone to take his stress away for one night.

A blonde caught his attention. She was making eyes at him, completely ignoring her friend. She'd do.

Andre approached her. "Hey."

She smiled. "Andre Stone, you sure have matured since the last time I saw you."

"I'm sorry. You have me at a disadvantage. You know who I am, but I don't know your name."

"Summer Richards. From Mr. Peters's class—high school biology."

"Oh! Summer. Now I remember," he lied. "You wanna dance?"

She smiled and giggled with her friend as she set her drink down. "Absolutely."

He held out his hand, and she took it. There was no current of electricity like when he'd touched Mia earlier. What had that been? Maybe he needed to get the wiring in the building checked.

Andre led his new dance partner onto the floor, doing his best to ignore his friend and Mia moving to the slow melody.

Summer wrapped her arms around his neck as they began to dance, spinning and swaying as his thoughts strayed.

Andre tuned out whatever she was saying, because Mia was laughing at something Bently had said, and his friend was holding her a lot closer than Andre was comfortable with. Acid burned his stomach.

"Did you hear me?" Summer asked.

"Uh, yeah. Me too." He hadn't really heard her, but it seemed like a good answer.

"Well, I'm glad you finally manned up and approached me," she said.

"Yeah, it was good to run into you. How's life been?" He was a bit rusty. The dating scene had changed in the last six years. How was he supposed to get from hello to her place again?

"I'd love to get to know you better. Do you want to go back to my place and do it in private?" She smirked like the cat that ate the canary.

So that was how it worked now—straight to the point.

He hesitated. He'd never been the one-night-stand kind of guy. Monogamy was his way of life.

Look how far that's gotten you.

Andre glanced up just in time to see Bently and Mia head towards the front door. Rage and unexplained jealousy coursed through his veins. He needed to get laid and stop obsessing over his neighbor.

"Sure."

Chapter 6

Mia

Rolling over in bed, Mia savored the soft cotton of her sheets against her bare skin. Opening her eyes, she searched the room. She got up and brushed her teeth before pulling on her running clothes and throwing her hair back in a ponytail. Her stomach grumbled as it always did when she ate greasy food the night before. Bently had been great company, offering to take her to dinner after their dance. He'd walked her to her car and wished her goodnight like the perfect gentleman.

Running into Bently and Andre was the last thing she had wanted when she went to The Shipwreck. She'd wanted to not drink alone for once. For some reason, returning home and noticing the empty driveway next door had stirred up a burning sensation in her chest. Heartburn from the greasy food most likely.

Mia drank a few sips of water before heading out the door for her morning jog. The first mile was slow as she moved sluggishly. She was off. Good thing she had a meeting with her therapist today. Her last half mile was met with the familiar sounds of footfalls thudding behind her. Anger flared as her guard went up.

This time he didn't pass, keeping pace with her from

behind. She grew impatient, feeling his eyes bore into her. She turned. Andre's glazed-over gaze was aimed at her ass. His eyes snapped back to the road.

"Enjoying the view?" she teased.

He grumbled and sprinted past her. If she had been keeping score, she'd have surely won this round.

* * *

Mia took an extra-long shower after her yoga before getting ready for the day. Even though she had no plans of leaving the house, she got dressed and did her hair. It helped her to stay motivated. One more tool in her toolbox when it came to fighting depression.

The familiar song of a Skype call sounded from her laptop. She clicked it open and greeted her therapist.

"Mia, it's so good to see you."

"You too, Dr. Martinez," Mia said.

"How have you been doing? How was the move?" she asked.

Mia smiled. "It's been mostly great." Mia caught her therapist up on the events of the last week, both the good and the bad.

"Sounds eventful."

"Yes," Mia agreed.

"Have you had any more of your blacking-out episodes?" the doctor asked.

Mia shook her head. "Not since the last time."

"What about panic attacks?" Dr. Martinez questioned.

Mia nodded. "Just one, but I know the trigger. Unfortunately, I can't avoid this one for the foreseeable future."

"Why not?"

Mia shrugged. "The man is a bully, but he happens to be my neighbor, my contractor, and the brother of one of my new friends."

"I see." Her therapist nodded, adjusting her reading glasses to perch on her nose. "Is it possible to find another contractor?"

Mia thought about it. Could she? She'd liked their work so far. They had been the only company willing to start right away, and for the best price. Plus, Remy was her friend, and to take business away from her husband seemed childish. "I'd rather not. I'll just do my best to avoid Andre. I don't know why he's so . . . ugh . . . I don't even know how to describe the way that man gets under my skin."

Dr. Martinez smiled. "Are you romantically attracted to this person?"

"He's hot. Like a ten out of ten. But the moment he opens his mouth, I just want to punch him in the face—not that I would." *Just knee him in the balls.*

"Okay, well, you know what to do to manage your panic attacks when they happen. It's best you try to minimize your contact with someone who isn't respecting your boundaries, or consider eliminating them from your life as much as possible. In the meantime, I want you to try and open up more with someone—one of your new friends perhaps? Share some things with them about yourself. I know personal sharing is hard for you, especially with your situation. But this can be simply what your dreams are or fond memories. Open up," Dr. Martinez instructed.

Mia swallowed, shifting uneasily in her seat. Her heart raced as she forced in a deep breath and nodded. "Okay. I will."

Mia said her goodbye and signed off.

Ding-dong. Mia closed the laptop and jogged down the stairs to peer out the peephole of the front door. Two smiling faces greeted her as she opened it.

"Hey, *chicas.* What are you doing here?"

Remy handed her a basket filled with two bottles of wine and baked goods. "We wanted to welcome you to the neighborhood."

"Come on in. Thank you so much. This is so kind of you." Mia accepted the basket as the women entered her home.

"No *pequeños*, little ones, today?" Mia asked.

"No, Mikel and Bently are on baby duty so we could have some girl time." Jasmine smiled, tucking a dark strand of hair behind her ear. Jasmine's almond-shaped eyes looked nothing like her brother's.

"*Perfecto.* You can help me drink these," Mia said, pulling the wine from the basket as she searched her drawer for a corkscrew.

"Don't mind if I do." Remy sighed as she sat in one of the barstools around the kitchen island.

"Please make yourself at home." Mia encouraged Jasmine, who had held back.

They poured their drinks, and the conversation flowed more easily as one bottle turned into two.

"I have to say, I have never done day-drinking before, but I think it's highly underrated." Mia chuckled.

"There isn't much opportunity for me as I'm almost always in mommy mode," Jasmine said tracing the rim of her glass with her finger.

"I don't usually drink more than one glass a couple times a year for special occasions, so I may be a little drunk right now," Remy said before she hiccupped.

The women all shared a laugh.

Mia patted Remy's thigh, about to say something, when the rough bump along her friend's skin drew her attention. She immediately retracted her hand, noticing the long scar. "I'm so sorry. I was just going to tell you that it means you have to spend the afternoon with me until you sober up," Mia said, hoping her apology was enough. She didn't mean to draw attention to her friend's injury.

Remy waved her hand. "Please don't worry." She pulled up her floral sundress to expose the full length of the healed dark flesh. "It's a long story, but basically there was an intruder in my home and I was the only person to stop him from going after my daughter."

Mia swallowed. Tears welled in her eyes. "*Dios mío*. I'm so sorry. I'm glad you and Lyra both made it out of that horrible situation." She wiped her eyes.

"We all have different things we've had to face. I like to think I came out stronger from it," Remy said, eyeing Jasmine. *Share something about yourself with your new friends. Open yourself.* Her therapist's words rang through her mind.

"That's why I started doing yoga," Mia blurted out.

"What's why?" Jasmine asked, seeming intrigued.

"To help with . . . trauma," Mia explained. Boy, when she decided to be more open, she went straight into the deep end. "It helps me connect my mind and body, to have something to look forward to, and to keep moving even when I feel . . . too depressed."

"Maybe it could help me," Jasmine said, her eyes meeting Mia's as an understanding passed between the women.

"When should we have our first session?" Mia laughed, trying to lighten the mood.

"Tomorrow at the beach. We're having a cookout at the cove," Remy said.

"It's a date," Mia agreed.

Was it too much to hope Andre wouldn't be there?

Chapter 7

Mia

The cool water was cleansing against her feet. Everything about the beach helped to ground her. The salty sea breeze and the wet sand between her toes. She closed her eyes, listening to the steady crashing of the waves as the tide began to recede. Seagulls cawed in the distance, most likely searching for scraps of food and other edible sea life.

"Okay, the guys have the kids, so we're ready to do this." Remy's voice approached from behind her. So far, she'd been lucky that Andre hadn't shown.

Mia opened her eyes and took in the sight of her two new friends. Remy's dark skin was stunning with the white bikini she wore in contrast. She didn't seem afraid to show the scar in the center of her thigh. Remy wore it more like a badge of honor—the mark of a warrior. If only Mia could be as open about hers.

"Yes. I'm excited to try this out." Jasmine's smaller frame fit snugly in an emerald-green one-piece that matched her eyes.

"I love that color on you," Remy said, motioning towards the red bikini Mia had thrown on with a pair of white shorts.

"Thank you. You both look stunning as always. *Hermosa*," Mia answered, walking towards the dry sand. She took a deep breath and centered herself as they made their way over to the yoga mats she'd already spread out for them.

"Choose a mat and sit in a comfortable pose." Mia sat and crossed her legs, demonstrating. She closed her eyes. "Bring your hands to your knees in any way that feels natural to you. I like to touch my pointer finger and my thumb together while keeping my palm facing up." After another moment, she explained, "Throughout our practice today, you must focus on your breath. Slow, steady four-count breaths."

They stayed like that for a few minutes, until she felt confident that Jasmine and Remy understood. Mia opened her eyes. "Lengthen your spine. You don't want to slouch. Reach the crown of your head towards the beautiful sun."

She guided them through the poses, giving them time to understand the positions, and reminded them to breathe slowly.

When they had finished, Mia was sweaty and ready to cool off. "Thank you for practicing with me," she said, bringing her hands to her heart. "Namaste."

"Wow. You wouldn't think these moves would be so challenging, but I have a feeling I'm gonna be sore in places I didn't know existed tomorrow," Remy joked.

"Thanks, Mia. I really enjoyed this." Jasmine smiled.

"I was just glad to have the company." She rolled her mat alongside the other two women before she walked over to their picnic table. Bently held baby Zoey, laughing as he pointed out their surroundings. Lyra was running from Mikel, giggling as he tried to catch her. Mia couldn't help the smile that came to her own face as she took the atmosphere in. These were her people—there was no doubt. For the first time since she'd lost her mother and left the only friends she had in the world back in California, she felt like a piece of home had been restored.

But then her eyes met his. Andre had shown up after all. He held Phoenix, his gaze targeted on her. She lifted her chin in defiance. She wouldn't give him the satisfaction of knowing how he affected her. She placed her mat in a pile, Remy and Jasmine following her lead.

"I've worked up an appetite. Is the food ready?" Remy asked Mikel as Lyra ran into her legs, clutching her mother for safety.

Flashes assaulted Mia's vision. The scent of her mother coated with fear as Mia clung to her. Only in Mia's memory, it wasn't a father chasing her in a child's game—it was a real monster.

"Ahhh! Mommy, save me," Lyra yelled, bringing her back to the present. Mia dug her feet farther in the sand as she focused on five things. Something she could see, hear, smell, taste, and touch. She grounded herself against the flashback.

"We've been kind of busy," Bently answered as Mikel caught his breath, motioning towards the baby in his arms.

"You could have worn her and started lunch. I'm starving," Remy complained.

"Here. Zoey probably needs to have some milk and take a nap anyway," Jasmine said, reaching her arms out to her daughter.

"I had Mikel set up those two umbrellas when we got here. It might be more comfortable for you to nurse there if you want," Remy said.

Andre stared at Mia in silence, anger radiating from him as he seemed totally oblivious to what was going on around him. The baby in his arms started to cry. *Even the child could sense his fury.*

"I'm gonna go for a quick swim," Mia said, turning around

and heading to the beach. She needed some air. Whenever Andre was in the vicinity, her chest grew tighter, making it harder to draw in a full breath.

Mia stepped into the cold water, wading out to her waist before she dove the rest of the way under. The water instantly cooled her and jolted her back into the present, erasing the tension that clung to her muscles. She didn't dare go farther in the water. She had a very real fear of sharks and not being able to see through to the sea floor. She turned and headed back to the shore. Her stomach sank. Andre was waiting at the edge, his arms crossed over his muscular chest. His scowl promised that this wouldn't be a friendly conversation at all. But when was it with this man?

She put her mask in place, walking to face him with her chin held high.

"Why are you everywhere I fucking turn?" he growled.

"*Perdóname?* I don't want to see you any more than you so seem to want to see me."

"These are my friends, not yours. You need to find someone else to hang out with," he snapped, taking a step closer.

She wouldn't be intimated by him. "Who do you think you are to dictate who I am friends with—or, for that matter, who your friends want to spend time with? Last I checked, you don't control me. No one does." She put her hands on her hips, defiantly.

His jaw clenched as her own anger rose. How dare he think he can just come over here and say these things to her. She had no one here, and he wanted to take the few good people in her life away.

"You know Bently probably won't want to see you again.

You're embarrassing yourself if you think he wants more. He's a one-and-done type of guy."

Her expression morphed into confusion. Andre thought she'd slept with Bently. Was he . . . jealous?

"Fuck you!" She was at her breaking point.

"No, thanks. You're not my type."

"You're a bully. And if you keep on treating people in your life like this, you're going to end up a sad and lonely man with nothing but regrets." She jabbed her finger at his rock-hard chest. The contact sent a jolt of electricity through her arm.

"I wasn't very lonely last night." He smirked.

Ugh! This man was infuriating! Everything inside her became untethered as she quaked with rage. *Two could play this game.*

"That makes two of us, then." She smirked.

His breathing became jagged as his eyes blazed with the intensity. "I don't care if you want to spread your legs for the whole goddamn town—just stay away from *my* friends."

"It's a shame someone as good-looking as you is so horrible on the inside." Mia twisted her face in disgust, the fire in her eyes blazing as she met him blow for blow.

"I could say the same about you," he growled.

"Oh, you like what you see? Take a good, long look, because that's all you'll ever get from me." She crossed her arms over her chest, knowing she was giving him a nice view of her ample cleavage. *So, this is the way to drive him mad.*

His eyes moved lower, caught in her trap. Andre's lips flattened as his eyes shot back to hers with a renewed disdain. He leaned closer to her face as he said, "I don't do sloppy seconds or desperate and, honey, you're both."

Her hand met his face with a loud *slap*. Mia's mouth gaped

open. Her face heated as her body trembled with an overpowering need to flee. Andre seemed just as stunned for a second before his gaze turned victorious. What the hell had she done? Since when had she become so physically violent?

Since Andre Stone.

Mia didn't like the version of herself that she became whenever he was around. Ashamed she had slapped him and angry that she let him get to her, Mia steadied herself with a shaky breath. She couldn't keep doing this. She had to get him out of her life.

"I want to terminate my contract with your company—effective immediately," she said.

His smile quickly faded, but her emotional turmoil over her actions and how she'd let him affect her muted any satisfaction. She turned quickly, fleeing from him.

* * *

Mia focused on the sand, searching for sea glass to keep her mind occupied. *Find the joy in all things. Look for the bright colors amidst the gray. Mija, there's always a rainbow after the storm. When the world is heavy on your shoulders, create your own happiness.* Her mother's words echoed in her mind as she fought back tears. How was she going to face Remy? She cared about the woman too much to put her in the middle of her hatred for her brother.

Lyra joined her a few moments later. "Mia! What are you doing?"

"I'm looking for sea glass." Mia held out her hand to show the little girl a few small pieces she'd found.

"Why? It's just broken bottles. That means it's garbage." Lyra scrunched her nose curiously.

Mia bent and picked up a piece of green glass that was still sharp around the edges. "You see this one?"

"Yeah," Lyra answered.

"This one isn't ready yet. Sometimes you can take something broken and shattered, something someone else would just throw away and treat like garbage, and turn it into something beautiful. It takes a lot of pressure. Waves must beat it against the sand and rocks, but eventually the jagged edges are smoothed and it becomes sea glass—something more beautiful than it started, and a whole lot stronger."

The little girl's eyes grew wide. "Can I have one?"

"Absolutely." Mia handed her the few pieces that she'd collected that were smooth before tossing the unfinished one back into the surf.

"How did you learn all this stuff?" Lyra asked, mesmerized by the rainbow of colors in her hand.

"My mamá used to collect sea glass. I still have a jar full of the colors she found."

"That's so cool! Isn't it, Uncle Andre?"

Mia tensed at his name. She glanced at him over her shoulder. His expression was one she hadn't seen on his face before—one of softness and possibly remorse. Could she never escape this man?

"Lyra, your mamá wants you to go eat. Lunch is ready," Andre said.

"Okay," Lyra said before she ran off.

"Mia—"

She held up her hand. "Don't talk to me. I don't want to hear it. Leave me alone, Andre. You won, okay? I'll keep to myself." She walked away before he could respond. Before he could see her tears.

Chapter 8

Andre

Andre followed from a distance as Mia headed up a trail on the side of the cliff. A few other people passed them on their way down. He had taken things too far with Mia. He couldn't explain his visceral reaction to her. Seeing her in downward dog in those tiny white shorts, her red bikini bottoms showing through, he'd lost it. Why he'd thrown Summer Richards in her face, he had no idea. He hadn't even made it inside the woman's house. *So why did I lie to Mia about it?* Images flashed in his mind of Bently's hands on her as they'd danced—as they'd left together. *Jealousy.* Now he'd really fucked up. *Mikel is going to kill me.* When did he become so selfish?

After following her and Lyra for a couple minutes, he couldn't help but overhear what she'd said about the sea glass. He got the feeling that maybe all that he sensed under the surface wasn't malicious lies or pretense, but a woman who'd seen her fair share of darkness.

When he reached the top, he found a small group of college-aged guys standing near the edge. Mia walked towards them and peered over the drop-off. This was a popular jumping spot for the locals and University of New Hampshire students. Mia took a step back, holding her head as if she was dizzy.

"Hey, beautiful," one of the guys with a fraternity Greek insignia cap said.

"Hey." She nodded.

"You up here to jump?" he asked.

She shook her head. "No."

"It's quite the rush. Watch. My buddy will show you how it's done," he said, putting his arm across her shoulder. His white skin contrasted with her dark tan. Andre was downwind from the guy, and he could still smell the beer on him, like he'd bathed in it.

One of the other guys ran and jumped off the ledge as she clutched her chest. The guy flipped and disappeared into the dark water below.

"It's a lot of fun," the drunk guy said.

"It doesn't look safe," she said, rubbing her arms.

"The water's like, mad deep, even with the tide out. Do I look like someone who would steer you wrong?" He smiled, showing off his perfectly straight white teeth. Men like him were used to getting what they wanted and never hearing the word no. Guys of that kind were the most dangerous.

"It's just not my thing." She shook her head and started to back away out of his grasp.

"Come on. I'll jump with you. The first time is always the hardest." He grabbed her wrist in a tight grip, not letting go when she tried to pull away.

"You're hurting me!"

"The lady said no," Andre barked. She turned, her expression seemingly relieved at the sight of him for the first time since they'd met.

"This isn't any of your business, thug," the guy said,

looking down his nose at Andre before handing off his hat to another one of the guys.

Andre's skin burned at the insult. Of course, there was only one reason the asshole would use that word. Andre's rage boiled over. He stepped closer. For once, his anger was directed at someone other than her. But they were outnumbered by four drunk white college boys and she stood perilously close to the edge of the cliff.

She tried to pull her arm free and shove the guy away, but Andre could tell she was being careful because they were so close to the edge.

"Fine. I'll let her go." The guy's face split into a cocky grin before he jumped off the cliff, pulling Mia with him.

Andre darted to the edge as Mia's scream intermingled with the jackass's shout before she plunged into cold darkness and the sea swallowed her up. His stomach hardened with nerves as he panicked.

He didn't wait for her to surface before he was free-falling himself, his heartbeat thudding in his ears. His only concern was her safety.

Mia erupted from the dark green waters a few yards away before he was plunged into the total darkness of the cold brine. He swam upwards, gasping for breath. He was closer to the frat boy who'd dragged Mia into the water, and as much as he wanted to punch the guy's face, Mia was his target. He swam as quickly as he could towards a panicking Mia. Tears streamed down her face. He wrapped his arm around her waist and guided her back towards the shore. Once he could reach the bottom, he pulled her against his body. The hard points of her nipples rubbed against his chest and sent a shiver along his spine. She'd lost her bathing suit top.

Shit.

He held her as she cried in his arms. Guilt ate him up from the inside out. The last thing this woman needed was him being an asshole to her.

"It's okay. You're safe." Andre led her away from the water onto the dry shore. He let her go long enough to peel the wet shirt from his body. "Here, take this."

He wrung it out as best as he could before slipping it over her head, looking away as she threaded her hands through it. She was trembling.

"See? Wasn't that worth it?" came the voice of the son of a bitch who'd dragged her off the cliff. Andre tensed, turning to face the cocky bastard, his fist clenched as he stalked back into the water towards him, ready for a fight.

A small hand gripped his bicep, halting him. "No, Andre," Mia said flatly. "He isn't worth it."

You're worth it.

Where the hell had that thought come from?

"Whoa, man. Listen to your girl. It was just a little fun," the guy taunted.

Andre jerked towards him, but Mia's hand only tugged him more firmly. "Let's go, Dre. He's not worth the assault charges."

Andre turned to Mia, her brown hair stuck to her skin, her nipples poking against the fabric of his shirt. He couldn't remember a more beautiful sight. She had him under her spell. It gave him the time to calm down. He'd probably get punished more harshly in front of a judge for punching this guy's lights out than the frat boy would for assaulting Mia. *What a fucked-up world we live in.*

Andre pulled Mia back into his chest as they walked away towards the beach with their friends.

"Th-thank you," Mia said, still shivering.

* * *

Bently seemed to know something was wrong the moment Andre locked eyes with him.

His friend came running over. "What happened?"

"There's a jackass frat boy over there who assaulted Mia. Threw her off the jumping ledge."

"I'll handle it," Bently said.

"Please don't get into a fight on my account. Really, I don't want you all to end up in jail because of me," Mia pleaded.

Bently laughed. "Honey, I'm the sheriff."

Mia's face paled. "I-I don't want to press charges. I just want to go home."

"I'll take you home. Bent, can you get my car back?" Andre asked.

"Yeah. You sure, Mia? It would really be my pleasure," Bentley pressed.

"I'm positive." Mia wrapped her towel around her body and gathered her yoga mats.

Andre ushered her to her car, helping her into the passenger seat. "You okay?" he asked.

She nodded.

He'd never seen her look so small and timid. In the short time he'd known her, she'd been feisty and full of energy. Pain laced through his chest. He was partly to blame. She'd have never gone up there if he hadn't acted like he did. His sister had been right—he was bitter.

"I'm sorry about before," he said.

No response.

He drove her home in silence. He put the car in park and jumped out to open her door. As he reached his hand to steady her, she pulled away.

"I can do it myself," she said. Some of the fire was back in her eyes.

"I know you can, but I want to help," he said as calmly as possible.

She unlocked her door and walked in, and he followed close behind her. Her house was a similar style to his. But her decor was colorful, warm and inviting, whereas his was more bachelor-pad chic with mismatched furniture and a few pictures and art pieces his mother had hung for him.

She stood there, staring at him, seeming so vulnerable. The mask she usually wore was gone. He stepped closer, unable to ignore the tether that cinched tighter between them, connecting him to her in a way he'd never felt before. Seeing her in danger had scared him more than he wanted to admit. The hurt in her eyes when he'd taken his tactics too far gutted him. Guilt clawed at his insides, along with an intense need to make it better, restore the light he'd snuffed out.

The pull between them was pure magnetism. He couldn't ignore it any longer. Placing his hand under her chin, he gently turned her face up to his. Need and lust tangled together with some unknown feeling. She was shaken up by the day's events, and he wanted nothing more than to wipe them from her memory, to make her feel good.

His lips hovered over hers, her sweet, hot breath tempting him, intoxicating him. If either of them moved, his lips would be on hers, devouring, tasting.

"I'm sorry for what I said and how I've acted towards

you. You do something to me and it makes me feel . . . out of control. I'm the one who lied to push your buttons. I never went home with anyone the other night."

She blinked before her eyes narrowed slightly. "Why tell me this now?"

Because you make me want things I shouldn't want. Because you should know you're nothing less than perfection.

"Little witch, your spell is beginning to work on me."

Shit, had he said that out loud?

A small sigh filtered through her parted lips.

The next moment, his mouth was on hers. A myriad of colors burst forth from inside his soul. She hesitated only a moment before returning his ferocity with her own. His tongue slipped into her mouth, warring with hers as he pulled her closer. Mia's teeth raked against his bottom lip, adding a pained pleasure to his experience. She moaned and his cock grew instantly rock hard, his swim shorts hiding nothing. He was an inferno, raging white-hot as her stiff nipples pressed against his bare chest. He ran his hands down the wet shirt that clung to her body. Andre was acting on impulse, and every cell in his body needed her naked flesh against his. He had to get inside her. As soon as his palms caressed the silky-smooth skin of her hips, he pulled her forward, grinding against her so that she could feel what she did to him.

Mia gasped, pushing him away. His arms immediately felt empty from the loss. They both stared at each other, panting. His body buzzed, every nerve ending firing, letting him know he was alive. One thing was crystal clear in this moment—he wanted Mia Garcia like he'd never wanted another woman, and the thought fucking terrified him.

Mia's eyes hesitantly searched his before she spoke, breaking the silence. "Thank you for helping me today. But, Andre, one good act doesn't erase all the bad. The things you said were beyond hurtful. I won't be treated that way by anyone." She backed away farther. "I'm sorry for what I said too. Even if it was the truth." She smirked. "I apologize for slapping you." She looked down, as if ashamed.

He nodded, accepting her rejection. She was right. He had acted like an asshole. "I'll need my shirt returned sometime. It's my favorite one." He winked.

She nodded. "Of course."

"Maybe you should sage yourself—get rid of the bad energy or whatever you called it, so you won't attract any more danger," he joked, trying to put a smile on her face.

Whatever he said backfired. Her expression morphed into pain before her mask was set firmly back into place.

"You want your shirt? Here," she said, just before she pulled the fabric over her head, exposing her perfect tan breasts and dark nipples. His cock shot to attention as all the blood in his head surged south.

"Lock the door on your way out," she said, turning and walking up the stairs out of his line of sight like she didn't just strip half naked in front of him.

Holy shit.

What. Just. Happened?

Chapter 9

Mia's letter

*T*o *the only man I've ever loved,*
I hope you can find it in your heart to read the words I have poured out on these pages. These are not excuses, but rather, an explanation. I must start from the beginning.

I can remember being six years old. Chasing mariposas *as my childish laughter tumbled from me like the weeds blown by the wind outside my parents' rancho on the edge of Montemorelos, Mexico. The sun was shining, warming my skin. I was so full of joy. I remember it so vividly because that's the last time I felt truly safe, like nothing bad could ever touch me. When I spotted the dust billowing in the distance, my belly did a summersault with excitement.*

Papi was home.

I ran back towards our red clay house to greet him. He'd been gone for two days and I was proud to report I'd fed the animals right on time like he'd requested, and with only a little help from Mamá.

As I neared his empty truck, my parents' voices drifted out from the kitchen. I drew closer, finding my father and mother both crying. Papi's face was covered in crimson. My mother tried to clean his wounds as I stood frozen, watching from the lattice. My father had never cried before, and the sight of his face immediately turned my blood to ice.

"If I don't give them the money they lost when the shipment was stolen . . ." he'd said.

I wish I could go back in time to that moment and ask him to finish that sentence.

Just days later, two men rode out to our ranch. They were clean and well dressed. One of them gave me candy. He struck up a conversation with me, telling me he had a puppy that he'd love to give to me if my papi said it was okay.

Papi had stayed inside since he returned. He'd even slept in the barn rather than our house which had seemed so strange to me. My childlike ignorance is a regret I'll carry with me to my grave.

The man asked if my papi was home. I'd been taught that lying was wrong, had it instilled in me since I could talk. So, I told the truth and it cost my father's life.

I had to watch as one man held my mother back while another led my father out of the barn at gunpoint. They asked him if he had the money and he said no. I later found out these men were from the cartel that forced my father to deliver shipments of cocaine when he moved cattle. In those parts, you either do what the cartel says, or you and everyone you love dies.

I watched, at six years old, as they put a bullet into my father's head. You might think that was horrific, but my story gets so much worse. I realize now they showed mercy to him in his death.

The men threatened my mother, saying if she didn't find a way to pay his debt, five hundred thousand U.S. dollars, that he'd be back for her and then he'd traffic me. The man who had pulled the trigger looked at me and said, "That little one attracts bad spirits, so I have a feeling we'll be seeing each other sooner rather than later."

After he left, my mother packed two bags and took all the money she'd saved behind a clay brick by the fireplace. We buried my father and waited until nightfall before we began the long and dangerous journey towards the border.

"The Americans will help us, mija. *We will seek asylum," she told me. That was the day my childhood ceased to exist.*

After what seemed like weeks of travel, most of it on an empty stomach and little water, my mother paid a coyote to bring us across the river. The way the man leered at Mamá made my stomach knot tightly. She paid him all the money she had. When we made it to the river, the man demanded more. My mother showed him her empty pockets . . . He said he would take other forms of payment. I clung to her, afraid she'd be taken from me too.

She forced me to stay put. "Close your ears, mija. *I'll be right back."*

It hit me all at once, the tears finally streaming down my face as I cried so hard no sound came out. I didn't obey; the grunts and whimpers from behind the rocks as my mother used the only currency available to save my life are permanently etched into my brain.

When we all climbed into the rickety raft, the water from the river quickly soaked our clothes. I must have still been crying because the man grabbed my neck and growled, "If you don't shut your mouth, I'll drown you in this river myself."

I've never told anyone this. Not even my therapist knows the extent of these details I'm sharing with you. I've never been this honest with any other person. The only reason I'm telling you this now is that you're not the only one who closed off to protect your heart. I love you, no matter what you think of me. You were right that you didn't know me, and this is me being more vulnerable than I've ever been before because I trust you.

Once we reached the border, hungry, tired, wet, and cold, we waited for the border patrol so we could turn ourselves in and apply for asylum. When their truck came into view, my mother cried with relief. I clung to her side, fearing everyone. If past events had taught me anything, it was that no one could be trusted.

Turns out I was right.

My mother was shoved by one officer, and verbally abused. They told us we'd be separated if my mother didn't give them the drugs they assumed she was smuggling. They told us to go back where we came from. My mother pleaded with them—the one English word she knew, "Asylum!" She repeated it over and over.

The officers had their chests puffed out. Sneering smiles of assumed dominance twisted their faces. They had their hands on their guns, like my mother and I were a threat to them. Power drunk, they grabbed my arm as I screamed for my mother. The one that held me laughed as tears leaked down my face. He put me in the back of his truck, alone and terrified.

Maybe that man who killed my father was right—I did attract the evil spirits. Bad energy. All I knew was that after everything we had been through, America's welcome was not what we'd expected. That should have been a sign of what was to come. That was the first time I wished I could be buried like my father. If life was this painful, I didn't want it to continue.

After what seemed like hours, my mother was handcuffed and seated next to me. Her face marred with dirt and streaks from her tears. I closed my eyes and leaned against her. I couldn't see my mother in any more pain when it was all my fault . . . for telling the truth.

Chapter 10

Mia

Mia sipped her coffee as she stared into her backyard. A dark shadow hovered above her like a storm cloud after the events of Saturday afternoon. She hadn't slept very well the last two nights because of it. Her fingers traced the seam of her lips. The passion of that kiss was unlike anything Mia had experienced before. Andre's lips were softer than she'd expected. His hands were rough and calloused from a lifetime of physical labor. She'd felt safe with him for a fleeting moment. He'd bullied her, pushed her beyond her limits, and then he'd saved her.

Why? A niggling feeling deep down told her that he was a good man, that his walls were only reinforced around her because he felt the energy between them. *Because he is scared.*

He'd offered her the temporary escape she craved. Why had she stopped him? Her body was certainly on board with the idea. Her self-worth, of course. What kind of message would it send to him if she gave in to the magnetic pull of their bodies while letting him treat her like crap? Obviously, it had been a good call. He'd opened his mouth and ruined the mood with his reminder that she attracted bad energy. Nothing could ever come of it anyway.

The doorbell chimed, and Mia set down her coffee as she went to answer it. She had just rolled out of bed, skipping her run this morning, opting for a day of doing nothing. Her anxiety was always higher after an event that triggered her. Being pulled off a cliff into the depths of a dark ocean with unknown creatures lurking around definitely qualified. Today was about self-care . . . and finding a new contractor, right after she called Mikel. The sooner she got this place done, the better. She was on a deadline with no room for error.

His dark bulky frame was evident behind the thick glass door. Andre was here. Drawing in a deep breath, Mia opened it, still wearing her silk pajamas.

Andre's eyes raked over her as he sucked in his bottom lip, biting down. He was in his running shorts without a shirt. Sweat beaded on his sculpted dark-brown chest. Mia squeezed her thighs together, trying to stifle the heat that blossomed there.

"Hey," she said.

"Can we talk?" he asked, meeting her gaze.

She nodded and walked inside as he trailed behind her and shut the door.

She pulled another mug from her cupboard. "Coffee?"

"Sure."

Mia filled the ceramic mug with hot liquid as she breathed in the earthy aroma. "How do you take it?" she asked.

"Black is fine."

Mia motioned to her barstool around the island and he sat as she set the steaming cup in front of him.

"Thank you," he said.

They both sipped their coffee in silence. Was he here about the kiss?

Andre set down his mug. "I wanted to apologize again about my behavior. It was unprofessional and well . . . I've been an asshole."

Mia smiled. "Thank you. I accept your apology. It seems we bring out the fire in each other."

"If you want me off the renovation, I'll stay away if it means that Mikel can keep you as a client. I was hoping you'd reconsider terminating the contract," Andre said, tracing his thumb over the rim of the coffee mug.

Oh, so this visit was about keeping his job, not the kiss.

She studied him while she thought it through. Had she overreacted? Could she give him one more chance? "If you continue to act professionally, and you respect my boundaries, I don't see why you can't have another chance. Despite our differences, your team is doing a great job from what I can tell."

Not to mention I really need this project finished at the agreed-upon date. October is right around the corner.

Andre's shoulders visibly relaxed as his lips turned up into a hesitant smile. "Thank you, Mia."

"You're welcome."

He stood. "Thank you for the coffee. I better head back so I can get to work on time. Wouldn't want my client unhappy." He smirked.

Was he flirting?

"Well, it's a good thing there are a few ways to make this one happy." She tested the waters.

Andre looked at her breasts. Unhelpfully, her nipples grew hard beneath the thin soft fabric, and his gaze. He bit his bottom lip again.

"I'll see you later," he said, before darting out the door.

Mia shook her head. She'd never met a more stubborn man.

* * *

Mia headed into the Stardust Café later that afternoon. She'd been craving one of Remy's lavender scones and finally given in. As she entered the café, the aroma of coffee and sweet pastries enveloped her senses, making her mouth water.

"Mia!" Remy excitedly greeted her as she walked from behind the counter to give her a hug.

"Remy. How is the café going?"

Remy released her. "I'm hanging in there. Business has picked up with the tourists coming through and wedding season upon us. I'm catering for an event this Saturday. How about you? I need to get your number. I wanted to check in on you but make sure it was alright before I stole your number from Jasmine."

"Oh, absolutely."

Remy pulled out her phone and Mia rattled off her number.

"I'm so sorry about what happened. I'm glad Dre was there to help." Remy offered her a friendly smile, putting the phone back in her pocket.

Mia's phone pinged from an incoming text. "Yeah, me too."

"Speak of the devil," Remy said, her focus on the doorway behind Mia. Mia turned, catching Andre's gaze as he approached them.

"Hey, big brother. You want the usual?" Remy asked.

"Yeah," he answered, not taking his eyes off Mia.

"What can I get you, Mia?" Remy asked.

"One of your lavender scones and a black coffee to go, please," Mia answered.

Remy got to work filling their orders, leaving them to wait. The whirring sound of the coffee machine and the low conversation of a few other guests were the only noises in the establishment.

After a few moments, Mia said, "I'm addicted to your sister's scones."

"She's a great baker." He rocked back on his heels and put his hands in his pockets.

There was more silence as his eyes looked anywhere but at her. *Okay, this is awkward.*

Remy rescued them by finally returning with coffee and bakery bags full of goodies. "Here you go."

Andre put a twenty-dollar bill on the counter as Mia dug in her wallet for a ten.

"Oh! Mia, I almost forgot. Sunday is Lyra's birthday party. We'd love it if you could come." Remy smiled up at her.

Mia looked to Andre. His eyes flickered. His words from a couple nights ago came back to her. He didn't want her around his friends.

"I'll have to see. I'm busy with a few projects, but go ahead and text me the details," Mia answered handing her the money before taking her items and leaving.

* * *

The rest of the week, Mia opted to work from home, avoiding Andre because that was what he'd asked for, but also because she got so confused around him. He was sending her mixed signals. Obviously, he was trying to be polite, but now it seemed almost unnatural. They just needed to have a conversation and clear this up. That kiss was the elephant in the room, and if he wasn't going to get to the bottom of this, she would. Mostly because her thoughts had strayed too much remembering the feel of his lips, and the taste of his tongue. The way he'd groaned when he . . . *Okay, enough.* She checked the clock. It was almost time for the guys to be done at the studio. If she left right now, she'd make it in time.

Mia walked into the future home of her yoga studio. The smell of sawdust and paint made it all so real. Pride squeezed her chest. She was actually doing this. On her own. She was making her dreams come true and honoring her parents' sacrifice.

"Hey, Miss Garcia," Tom said.

"Good evening. How is your family doing?"

"Great. Thanks for asking. You looking for Mikel? He's already left for the day. I'm about to head home myself." He shrugged the tool belt over his shoulder. "Andre's the only one here. He's in the room that will be your office."

"Okay, thanks. Have a good night." She nodded.

"You too," Tom said before he walked out the door.

Mia walked down the hall, taking in the changes she'd missed that week. Almost every area had been sheetrocked and mudded.

The door to the office was open, the light on as Andre sat in a folding chair, flipping through a stack of papers. His work pants were covered in little white specks of what she assumed was mud. His hands had white bits of the plaster contrasting with his dark skin. The evidence of his hard day's work all over his body did her in. It reminded her of all the times her father came in from a long day on their ranch. Her mother would pull off his boots and wash his feet. In turn, he'd do the same for her. Their marriage was a partnership, both working hard to build a life for Mia.

Andre glanced up at her, as his hands stilled. "Did you need something?"

Oh, right. The fact that she couldn't get him off her mind and she needed an outlet for all the stress in her life.

She walked the rest of the way into the office as he stood, setting the papers on the chair behind him.

"Yeah, I wanted to talk to you about last weekend," she answered, stepping closer. She searched his eyes, hoping he'd understand.

"Which part?" he asked, staring at her mouth.

Yes, that one.

"You kissed me." Her voice came out breathier than she'd intended.

Andre bit his bottom lip. His chest rose and fell more rapidly.

Mia ran her hand over the side of his jaw, the electricity immediately flowing. "Do you feel this energy between us too?" She wasn't asking for anything except sharing their bodies. That was all she could afford to do anyway. The chemistry of the kiss promised an experience she wouldn't regret. She needed that escape.

"Yes," he said, though it was part tortured groan.

She leaned her mouth closer to his, waiting for him to make the decision, to give in to the lust-fueled fire between them.

"But . . ." he said, his words tickling her sensitive lips.

"But?" she asked.

"It was a mistake in a moment of weakness and it won't happen again," Andre said, stepping back from her, every muscle tense. The lust was still evident in his eyes as his walls were reinforced.

Her anger and frustration rose. "Why are you punishing yourself?"

"I'm just not into you like that," he defended.

"Your eyes say different. The way you kissed me tells me you're a liar. What would have happened if I didn't stop that kiss?" she asked.

His jaw clenched as he stared at the drop cloth on the floor, not responding.

He left her hanging. How had she ended up embarrassed and vulnerable by this man again? She needed to take control of the situation and protect her pride. "You want to play indifferent? Fine. You wanted space? I'll give you that too." She turned to storm out, but he grabbed her arm. She faced him, anger blazing through her as she waited for his response.

Andre didn't move, his posture growing even more rigid. It was as if the man were made of stone.

"What?" she yelled.

He winced. "I told you to stay away from my friends—"

"Ugh! *Eres mas terco que una mula!*" Mia said as she yanked her arm away and stomped out of her studio to her car.

The man was insufferable.

Chapter 11

Andre

Inhaling a deep breath, Andre made his way through the grass towards his sister and Mikel's house with a gift under his arm. He searched the driveway. *She's not here.* Would she still come after their blowup? It had been a long time since he'd taken Spanish in high school, but he caught "stubborn" and "mule." Just remembering how feisty she'd been made his own blood heat with arousal. Damn. They had some sizzling chemistry between them. Too bad it couldn't ever happen.

Andre didn't bother with the doorbell, and he went right in.

"Uncle Andre!" Lyra said, running up to him with her arms wide open. Children were so trusting and pure. *Then we grow up and life teaches us not to trust.* Andre's brow creased as he pushed the thought away.

"Hey, birthday girl."

"Is that for me?" she asked as she jumped up and down in excitement.

"Sure is, sweet pea." He handed over the present.

"After cake you can open it, right, Lyra?" Remy said as she approached them.

"Awww alright. I'll put it with the others." His niece skipped off.

Andre followed Remy to the backyard where his parents were chatting with Mikel, and a few other little kids ran around with Lyra. Jasmine sat while Zoey lay on a blanket, with the sun shining on their small gathering.

"Where's my nephew?" Andre asked.

"Napping." Remy motioned to the baby monitor on her hip. "Food's ready. Everyone help yourselves," Remy called.

Andre grabbed a plate and filled it up. He was never one to pass up a home-cooked meal.

A large hand slapped his back roughly. Andre turned as Bently smiled.

"Hey, buddy, save some for the rest of us." Bently chuckled.

"Nah, you look like you could use a diet," Andre joked.

Bently feigned a hurt expression as he clutched his heart. "Hit a guy where it counts. I'm as in shape as I've ever been."

Images of Bently at the end of his battle with cancer filtered through Andre's mind. His best friend had been through a lot and came out stronger.

"I just mean you look healthy, bro."

Bently sighed and looked away. "I'm healthy as a horse." Something was bothering him, but he'd been so private about the whole ordeal, Andre didn't even know what kind of cancer his friend had had.

"You know I'm here if you ever need to talk. Right, man?" Andre offered.

"I'm fit as a fucking fiddle. Promise." Bently winked.

"I'm just saying. I'm not goin' anywhere."

"Can't believe our niece is seven. Can you?" Bently asked, changing the subject.

"Seems like just yesterday we were helping Remy with her as a baby," Andre admitted.

"Thankfully Mikel knew what was good for him and came back," Andre said.

Remy approached them as Bently said, "If my brother hadn't gotten his head on straight, who knows? Maybe I would have married your sister."

Remy laughed. "You think I'd want the town man-whore?"

"Hey, now! Baby, you're the type of woman who could make a man like me settle down." He grabbed her hand and pulled her into his lap as she squealed.

"You just like my cooking," she argued.

"Well . . . that too," Bently conceded.

"She's taken," Mikel growled as he walked towards them, extending a hand to his wife.

Remy stood back up, her husband possessively wrapping his arms around her.

"Come on, bro. Maybe we could share. We could be brother-husbands." Bently smirked.

Andre shook his head. Bently never stopped. "It's a good thing your brother knows you're full of shit."

"I don't share." Mikel smiled and kissed Remy hard on the lips, his hands wandering to her backside as he lifted her against him.

"Come on, now. This is a kids' party—your kid. Keep it PG, man. No matter how long you two are together, she's still my sister."

Mikel turned to face him as his grin widened. "If I had listened to you the first time you told me that, we wouldn't have the birthday girl herself."

Bently erupted in laughter as Andre shook his head, trying to hide his smile. Seeing his best friend and his sister so happy brought the familiar pang of pain, knowing he'd never have that. He could never trust another woman like that again, and a union without trust was no relationship at all.

The cake was cut and the birthday girl opened all her gifts. Where was Mia? Guilt weighed heavily on his shoulders. He'd kept her away from this, and she was all alone. Maybe it was for the best if they stayed apart from each other. They were like fire and gasoline, and the only thing that could come from that combination were ashes of destruction.

Lyra ran up to him with the Katherine Johnson Barbie doll he'd gotten her. "Uncle Andre! Thank you so much for my present. I love it!" she squealed, holding the doll close to her chest with a yoga mat decorated with the solar system in the other hand.

"Did I get the right one?" he asked.

"Yes. Did you know Katherine was the woman who used math to help the astronauts get home safely from their trip to the moon? She was like a human computer she was so good at math. Mommy says if I want to be an astronaut, then I have to learn a lot of math too." Her words came in rapid succession.

"Well, I guess you better get to it, then, huh?" He tugged on one of her long braids. "Who gave you the yoga mat?" Andre asked, searching the small crowd once more.

"Mia!" Lyra yelled as she ran back to her grandparents.

Mia is here? Where?

"She came this morning before the party started to drop off the gift," Remy said from behind him.

Andre turned to face her. Phoenix nursed from the carrier tied around his sister.

"Oh." He nodded.

"Look at you trying to pretend your eyes haven't wandered

to my back door every five minutes since you got here." She laughed.

"I have not." Had he?

"What is stopping you? Mia and I have hung out a few times, and I think she's a genuinely good person. She's been through a lot. She lost both her parents." Remy continued, but Andre got caught on that one detail. She'd lost her parents? He'd called her a spoiled princess that day, making some stupid comment about her mother and father spoiling her before she'd run off on the verge of tears. What a fucking idiot!

"You were right. I was mean to her. I apologized already. But, Remy, I'm not looking for a relationship." *Ever.*

"Say that first part again, please?"

He rolled his eyes. "You were right."

She smiled. "Wow, Andre Stone. I never thought I would hear those words from you."

"Don't get used to it."

"You know you could have saved a lot of heartache if you'd listened to me and Bently about Tiffany. We told you the woman wasn't good for you," she said.

It was like he'd been addicted to Tiffany—the highs, the lows—a ride he couldn't get off. They'd burned hot and then it just fizzled. But he'd stayed with her out of obligation and because of the chemistry when things did happen to go right.

"The heart wants what the heart wants." And that was precisely why he needed to stay away from Mia. His heart and body wanted her, but his mind knew better. If he gave into the chemistry again, he'd probably end up at the same dead end he had with Tiffany.

"I'm just saying, all your friends like Mia. She's nothing

like Tiffany. You should open up and give her a chance," Remy argued.

"Can we stop bringing up my ex?"

"Fine."

"I gotta go anyways. Got some stuff to catch up on," Andre said.

"You should bring a piece of cake to Mia," Remy said.

Yeah, right.

* * *

Later that afternoon, Andre shut the mower off, the smell of fresh-cut grass mixing with the gasoline from the machine. He parked it in his shed before walking back to his house, glancing over to Mia's before he entered. That kiss they'd shared was seared on his brain, and no amount of running or lawn mowing could shake it.

He ran up the stairs for a shower. Heading out to his balcony, he took a few moments as the warm breeze filtered past him. His eyes wandered to Mia's backyard. She too was outside on her back porch, white curtains billowing from the wind behind her. Her tan body shimmered in the sunlight. Her hair was slicked back from what he assumed was a swim. A light purple towel wrapped around her, showing off her beautiful toned legs. Andre stood unmoving, enraptured by the sight before him. She sat right at the edge of the back porch. Mia held a picture frame in her hands as her shoulders began to quake and she wiped her eyes. She was crying. His lust quickly turned into a mix of curiosity and guilt. Was it his fault? Was she lonely because of his stupidity?

As much as he wanted to comfort her—craved it, really— he couldn't do that because there were only two possible outcomes with Mia: fighting or fucking—with her, probably both. Andre couldn't afford to get close to Mia. He needed to protect himself. He walked inside and got in the shower, ignoring the pull towards the last woman in the world he should want.

Chapter 12

Mia's letter

*L*ife in America was so different to life in Mexico. My mother found work cleaning for fourteen hours a day while I was enrolled in school. I didn't speak a word of English, but thankfully our neighbors at the motel we lived in quickly became friends. Mateo and Carmen helped me learn the language and navigate the education system. They are still my best friends to this day. Their mother would check on me from time to time. They didn't have much either, but she always offered me food when I was in their room.

One day, I came home from school after a particularly bad day of being bullied for my accent. My mother was in between shifts at one of her many jobs that paid her well below minimum wage. She took one look at me and suggested we make her polvorones. We searched the almost bare cupboards for the ingredients and chatted in Spanish about good times in the past with my father—memories that brought laughter. She dropped a powdered cookie in my hand with her calloused fingers and said, "These are best when made with love and laughter. Don't believe what anyone says that's negative about your heritage, because you're not anything less than beautiful."

I remember the day we received the letter from the government denying us asylum. Because the cartel had demanded money from us that we couldn't pay, the U.S. government considered our plight 50 percent economic hardship, which made us ineligible for asylum.

It was the first time my mother didn't cry when bad news came. It was as if she had been through so much trauma that she'd run out of tears to grieve. I had wondered if there was a set amount of tears a person could cry in their lifetime. When would my mamá get a break, and be able to be free and happy again like we were with Papi on the ranch? I wished she would get that peace, prayed to all the saints who would listen, even mother Mary herself. If only I'd known that death would be the only form of peace for her—I'd take back all my prayers. I'd do so much differently.

Living as an undocumented person in the United States was difficult to say the least. My mother made yearly trips to check in with Immigration and Customs Enforcement facilities. To go back to Mexico was a death sentence. We'd received letters from the cartel. They knew where we lived and sent detailed threats on how they would end our lives. The U.S. government had copies and they still denied us refuge, even though we followed the legal route towards asylum.

I applied for DACA (Deferred Action for Childhood Arrivals) and because of that was granted a social security number so I could work and go to college, and get a license.

Everything was going okay. I was determined to get my degree and make a better life for my mother so she wouldn't have to be in so much pain from working herself to death. But then the elections came, and the new president who'd promised to only deport criminals was tearing families apart. I lived in terror that when I came home from school, my mother would be taken from me without a word. That ICE officers would invade my classroom and take me out in handcuffs. Anxiety and nightmares made it hard to sleep and function as a freshman in college.

This is what my life as a Dreamer (an undocumented person permitted to live in the U.S. since they were brought in as a minor) was like. This *is why I don't share about myself, because I could be turned in at any moment and sent back to Mexico. This is life or death for me.*

I tell you this not to make an excuse for my lack of openness, but to give you an explanation that this rift is me, not you. It is my fault, all of it. Both my parents' deaths, and the way things ended between us.

Chapter 13

Mia

Hot tears ran down Mia's cheeks as she stared at the picture of her mother.

"*Feliz cumpleaños, Mamá.*" Mia brought the glass of tequila to her lips. This was her mother's second birthday since she'd been ripped from this world. It didn't seem any easier than the last.

"You wouldn't want me to be sad on your birthday. I'm the only one left to honor you, and I'll do it right. I'll make a feast and we'll have a party." Mia sniffled as she carried the picture frame inside with her glass in the other hand.

After setting it on the counter, she played one of her mother's favorite songs—"*La poller colorá*" by Carmen Rivero y su Conjunto. As the familiar sound wound around her, it took her back to the many times she'd danced in the kitchen while her mother made tamales. Her neighbor and best friend, Lucia Lopez, together with Carmen and Mateo, had always helped in preparation for Christmas. The red pomegranate on the counter caught her attention as an idea struck.

Mia pulled out poblano peppers from the fridge, along with all the other ingredients she would need. Luckily, she had some leftover slow-cooked pork that would do just fine. She got to work preparing *chile en nogada*—one of her mother's favorites.

Sometime later, her phone rang, silencing the music. Mia washed her hands quickly before answering. "Hello?"

"*Hola, mija. Cómo estás?*" Lucia asked.

Mia answered her in her native tongue as they continued in Spanish. "I am doing well, Señora Lopez. How are you?"

"I miss my other daughter. When can I come and see the new place you have for yourself?" she asked.

"Give me another month or two and you guys can fly out to see it when it's all finished," Mia said.

"Alright. How are you doing? I know this day is hard for you. Your mother was a strong and courageous woman," Lucia said, pride mixed with her own grief apparent in her voice.

Mia's eyes stung as more tears gathered. She picked up her glass and downed the rest of her tequila before pouring herself some more. "It's still hard, but I will honor her and celebrate her life. I'm making *chile en nogada.*"

"Her favorite!" Lucia said.

"Yes."

"She would be so proud of you, *mija,*" Lucia said.

Mia swiped the tear that fell down her cheek, the open wounds of her grief bleeding out with slices of regret. Every heartbeat pained her as guilt weighed heavily on her shoulders.

"I won't let her and Papi's sacrifices be for nothing." Mia swallowed the ball of emotion rising in her throat.

"Ahhh, *cariño,* your life and your freedom is all they cared about. You live and be happy. That's the only thing your mother wanted. She reminded you all the time," Lucia said, her voice comforting. The woman was the closest thing she'd ever have to family.

"I remember." Mia's lips curved into a watery smile.

"Now, go make that delicious food, and don't forget to have a glass of tequila for her. You know how much she loved celebrations." Lucia chuckled.

"I will."

"Invite your neighbors and friends you've made there. I'm sure you can find someone to share this day with," Lucia said.

A pang of hurt added to the turmoil in her chest. She couldn't invite her neighbor—he'd made it perfectly clear he wanted nothing to do with her. And with no desire for more drama with Andre, she didn't want to invite his friends who were quickly becoming hers. Besides, today was Lyra's birthday as well, and she wouldn't interrupt their family plans. No, she'd do this alone—like everything else.

"Sure," Mia answered to appease her second mother.

"Well, I'll let you get to it. *Buenas tardes, mi amor*," Lucia said.

"*Adíos*," Mia said before hanging up.

She sighed as the music automatically started again, the song far more cheerful than she felt. She took another sip of the tequila. "*Salud, Mamá.*"

Chapter 14

Andre

Later that night, Andre pulled the car into his driveway. The festive music blaring from his neighbor's house immediately made him tense. All the lights were on in her house and the windows open, only making it that much more obnoxious. There was no way he would be able to sleep with that noise blaring. He checked his watch—ten thirty. There was a noise ordinance in their neighborhood, and in sixty seconds she'd be breaking it.

"Fuck it," he said, heading straight over to her door. There was no way she'd hear a polite knock over the loud music, so he pounded his fist against the door. He waited and waited. Pounding the wood again, his impatience grew. Did she have company?

Finally, the door opened, the music growing louder as it bled out into the night. Her dark hair spilled over her naked shoulders. The red dress she wore glittered in the moonlight—her long tan legs and curvy thighs on display for his viewing pleasure. She was barefoot, and for some reason it made him smile.

"This is the very opposite of space!" she yelled over the music as she hiccupped.

He'd been caught checking her out. There was no mirth in her expression. Her eyes were glassy and red.

"I can't hear you over the music!" he shouted back.

She turned, slightly swaying as she walked away towards the kitchen and dialed down the sound until it was nothing but a soft background noise.

Something smelled amazing. His mouth watered as he followed her inside and shut the door.

She drained clear liquid from a glass and poured more from the near-empty liquor bottle. That explained the swaying.

"What is all this?" he asked, sitting in the same seat he'd taken when he'd visited before.

"It's my mother's birthday today," she said as a beeping from the oven went off. She slipped on a pair of mitts and leaned a little too far left as she opened the oven.

He winced and shot to his feet. She was going to hurt herself. "Let me help."

She pushed him away with one of her covered hands. "I don't need your help. I can do it all by myself."

Her bloodshot eyes bore into him. The pain reflected back sliced him to ribbons. *Grief.* He slowly backed away and took a seat again.

Mia pulled out a pan before removing the lid as steam rose around what looked like stuffed peppers of some sort. She grabbed a handful of red pomegranate seeds from a bowl on the counter and sprinkled them on top, her hands staining pink.

"Remy told me your parents passed. I'm sorry about what I said before," he said.

She turned and faced him, leaning against the counter like she needed the support. "You sure are sorry for a lot of things."

He chuckled. "Only when it comes to you."

A moment of silence passed as they gazed into each other's eyes. Every cell in his body wanted to pull her into his arms and make her forget everything for a little while. He wanted to make her feel good.

"So that's what smells so delicious?" he asked.

"*Chile en nogado*. It was my mother's favorite. It is believed that the nuns who prepared a feast for Augustin de Iturbide after he signed the Declaration of Mexico made up the dish to incorporate the colors of the Mexican flag—green, red, and white," she explained, and sweet baby Jesus, her accent alone was enough to turn his cock to steel.

"You're celebrating solo?" he asked. The hurt that flashed in her eyes made him want to retract the question. Of course she was—he'd kept her away from Remy and Jasmine.

"I don't have anyone else." Her voice was quiet as the room grew more somber. Her words were like a punch to his gut.

"Well, you're not alone now," he said. "That is, if you want my company at all?"

She blinked and turned away, facing the window to her backyard.

"I guess that's my cue to leave," he said, standing. Her shoulders trembled as if she was crying. *Oh, Mia.* He strode over, and took her in his arms. She leaned against him, quietly crying. He wished more than anything he could fix this. "I'm sorry," he said, unsure of what else would bring her comfort.

She sniffled and backed away enough to look him in the eyes. "You must think I'm *loca*."

"No more than the rest of us. I can't imagine losing my mother, much less both my parents."

She looked down.

"Do you want to talk about them?" he offered.

She hesitated, before asking, "Are you hungry?"

"Yeah."

"Are you allergic to nuts?" she asked.

He shook his head.

"Take a seat." She sniffled and reached into the cupboard, pulling two plates down. He followed her movements as she plated the food. She was focused, and the silence was easy between them for the first time. Some sort of Spanish music was still playing in the background as his stomach grumbled.

She set the food in front of him with a fork and knife before placing hers next to him on the corner of the island. Mia poured him a drink from the tequila bottle and then raised her glass. He did the same.

"*Salud*," she said.

"*Salud*," he repeated.

The first bite was a bit hot. The flavors exploded on his palate. The savory, nutty dish had just the right amount of spice with tartness from the crunchy pomegranates. "This is the best thing I've ever had in my mouth," he said.

"That's because you've never tasted me."

His mind went blank as he coughed and reached for his drink. The alcohol burned his throat as he gulped it down.

"Are you okay?" she asked, patting him on the back. Heat spread from her touch, the blood rushing to his groin. Surely he was hearing things.

"*Dios*, did I say that out loud? I think I've had more tequila than I realized." Her cheeks blushed red as she took another drink.

"You want to tell me about your mom?" he asked, switching the subject as he adjusted himself in his seat. He should have changed into sweatpants before he came over, instead of the restricting jeans. Now all he could think about was tearing off her clothes and tasting the nectar between her thighs.

"Mamá was the strongest woman I've ever known." Mia began as she picked up the picture frame from the counter he hadn't noticed before.

A woman gazed back with Mia's eyes, Mia's smile.

"She's beautiful," he said.

"She was. She worked so hard to make a life for me here," Mia explained, her brow creasing as if it was an unpleasant memory.

"She immigrated from Mexico?"

Mia nodded.

Okay, so getting her to talk was like pulling teeth.

"Do you mind if I ask how she died?"

Mia's eyes grew dark and vacant as if she was no longer present with him.

"You don't have to—"

"A fire," she said quietly.

"I'm sorry."

Mia nodded. The vast pools of her eyes glazed as if her mind was a far way off.

He shifted the conversation. "I took some Spanish in high school. I don't remember much, but I can pick up a few words and phrases."

"Oh yeah?" She turned her attention back to him as a small smile curved her face.

"Enough to know you said something about me being a stubborn mule the last time we talked." He chuckled.

Her face morphed into a full smile, the light coming back

to her eyes. "Well, you are. It's the truth, and you made it clear you only wanted the truth."

"I wanted to let you know I was wrong. You don't have to stay away from my friends, and I won't give you a hard time about it." He ate another bite.

"Do you apologize to other people as much as you do me?" she asked as she studied him.

"Nope. There's something about you that brings out parts of me I didn't know existed. Things I've never felt before," he admitted.

She leaned closer. "I can think of a lot more parts for us to explore together."

The energy crackled between them as he clenched his jaw. The alcohol was weakening his defenses. Why shouldn't he just give in? What were his reasons again?

She must have taken his silence for a refusal, because she drank down the rest of the liquid in her glass and stood. "Dance with me, *por favor?*"

It was then the slow sensual music was brought back to his attention. Touching this woman was a bad idea. But he couldn't tell her no—not when she seemed so vulnerable and breakable. He'd caused her enough pain with his misguided attempts at self-protection.

Andre stood, taking her hand and spinning her around. His chest tightened as a smile adorned her face. She was breathtakingly beautiful. He pulled her close, her body melding perfectly against his. She swayed and moved her beautiful figure hypnotically to the rhythm. Her movements were sensual and confident as her dark eyelashes fluttered closed. His knee wedged between her thighs ever so slightly.

Each moment of contact became more and more

overwhelming. His cock was so hard it was burning with the need to be inside this woman. Mia turned, her perfect plump ass grinding against his groin, adding fuel to the fire. Her arm wrapped around his neck as they danced, cheek pressed to cheek. His body was an inferno, raging with desire for her. Andre pressed his hands into her hips, forcing her closer in exquisite torture. Every nerve ending fired, his body pulsing from the pent-up need. He was going to come in his pants like a fucking teenager if this didn't stop. He grabbed her arm and spun her back around so that she was facing him. He was panting now. It was agony to deny his body any longer.

"*Quiero que me chingues hasta olvidar todas mis preocupaciones,*" she said, her voice breathy and needy.

I want you to fuck me and make me forget all my worries.

Maybe he wasn't so rusty with his Spanish after all.

All thoughts left his mind as overwhelming, uncontrolled lust slammed into him. Her scent was intoxicating, poisoning his self-control. He captured her face in his hands.

It was over. He'd given in.

He was going to kiss Mia, and then he was going to do just what she'd asked until she was so overcome with pleasure that she pleaded for him to stop.

"*Si, hermosa.* Anything you want."

There was no way he could be gentle—he'd waited far longer for this moment than he cared to admit. He leaned in, his mouth watering with anticipation of her sweet lips on his.

Mia's eyes grew wide as she slammed her hand against her mouth.

Andre frowned in confusion as she ran out of the room, the sound of gagging following soon after.

Shit.

Andre went after her, holding her hair back as she threw up the contents of her stomach into the toilet. He used one hand to grab a purple towel, and wet it in the sink before handing it to her to wipe her mouth when she'd finished.

"Please, just go," she begged. "This is so embarrassing."

"I know I haven't been the best example of it lately, but my mama raised me right. Let me help you to bed," Andre said.

Mia nodded as she wiped her mouth again and stood.

Andre held on to her arm and guided her up the stairs towards her bedroom. He slipped into the bathroom and found two pain pills and a glass which he filled with water. Mia followed him inside where she brushed her teeth before accepting the glass.

He held her hand as they walked to her bed, setting the pain pills by the refilled glass for the morning. Just twenty minutes ago, he'd thought he'd be seeing her bedroom for other reasons. How had he let it get that far?

"Can you unzip my dress?" she asked, tucking a lock of her dark hair behind her ear.

The woman was beautiful even in her brokenness—like shattered stained glass glittering in the sunlight in a mosaic of colors. That was why. This woman was so stunning, it made him weak in the knees.

Andre swallowed and took his time, exposing her soft tan flesh. The fabric dropped to the floor, leaving the black lace underwear she had on underneath and nothing else. The image would be forever burned in his mind. Mia crawled into her bed, covering herself with the floral comforter. Her hair splayed out on the pillow and he couldn't stop the flash of disappointment he felt at leaving her like this.

He leaned down and kissed her forehead. "Sleep well."

"*Gracias, mi héroe.*"

Her hero? He'd be a liar if he didn't admit that he wanted to be whatever she needed. When had that happened?

Since he'd let his heart make the decision.

Her soft breathing signaled she was asleep as she curled herself into a ball on her side. He walked downstairs and began to tidy the kitchen. He couldn't do this. Mia hadn't said much, but he recognized the broken look in her eyes. Last time, he'd made the mistake of trying to be a hero for his ex, and look how that had turned out. She'd used him and then left him an empty shell with nothing remaining. He couldn't go through that again. Mia could be his friend and nothing more.

"I can't be your hero, Mia."

Chapter 15

Mia

Pulling open the front door, Mia breathed in the dewy, early morning air. She felt like crap, but she believed it was better to sweat out the hangover than wallow in it. She glanced down. A plate with a piece of cake and a note had been left on her porch. She lifted it, carrying it inside as she read the note.

Every birthday party should have cake.

Mia smiled and placed it inside before heading out for her morning jog.

As she made her way around the neighborhood, she kept checking over her shoulder for Andre. He caught up with her at their usual crossover point.

"*Buenos días,*" she greeted.

"Good morning to you," he said, keeping pace with her.

"Thank you for last night." She'd told him to fuck her and then nearly thrown up all over the man. After all that, he'd left her cake. She smiled. That warm feeling bubbled up in her chest.

"It's no problem. I'd do it for any of my *friends*."

He'd made sure to emphasize *friends*. She sensed whatever

progress they'd made last night had been flushed down the toilet too. He was so hot and cold.

"Is that what we are? Friends?" she asked, carefully.

"That's all we can ever be," he panted, his chest heaving up and down as he gulped in air.

She couldn't help the disappointment that squeezed her heart. Not to mention the embers of lust left over from remembering how it felt to have his body so close to hers last night—knowing that if she hadn't gotten sick, he'd have been in her bed.

"Wanna race back?" She smiled.

He laughed, out of breath. "Sure. Ready, set—hey!"

Mia laughed as she charged ahead before he called it. She pushed herself as her legs burned. His heavy footsteps caught up to her and she swerved in front of him. Her driveway was only another three yards away—she could make it.

"Whoa! Cheater," he called, quickly maneuvering around her.

She grabbed on to his arm, endorphins mixing in a cocktail with the energy that sizzled between them. As she laughed for real for the first time in a long time, warm joy filled every cell of her body like rays of sunshine lighting her from the inside out. The feeling of freedom enveloped her.

Andre stopped abruptly, pulling her backwards as he spun them around so that he was closer to their homes.

"Hey! Let me go so I can win," she teased between fits of giggles.

He backed up, holding her in front of him. She couldn't advance past him.

"No way. You cheated," he said, out of breath, a smile playing across his lips.

"You're in better shape than me. I just took an extra few seconds' head start so it would be fair," she argued. Her skin burned as he raked his gaze over her.

"I think your shape is perfect."

Butterflies tumbled in her belly, still drunk on tequila fumes. "Careful, Mr. Stone, those aren't things friends say to each other . . . unless."

"Unless what?" he asked.

She took the leap. "Unless they're friends with benefits."

He stopped walking, staring at her intently as if he was making the most difficult decision of his life. A flash of rejection formed in his eyes, and she didn't want to be turned down again. She wouldn't beg anymore for this man.

Mia darted around him, crossing the finish line first. "I won!"

Andre shook his head, moving his hands to his hips. His grin widened. "Next time, I'll know your tricks and beat you."

"We'll see, won't we?" She laughed, heading into her house.

* * *

Later that afternoon, Mia arrived at The Lighthouse Inn. She carried in a small box of supplies while Jasmine held the door open for her.

"Hi, Mia. I'm so glad you could come over. Zoey's napping, so it worked out perfectly," Jasmine said, closing the door behind them. The foyer was open and simple, with white paneled walls and polished wood floors.

"I'm just glad to have something to do and get out of the house," Mia said, following her friend up the grand staircase. "This inn is beautiful."

"Thank you. I used to help take care of the woman who

lived here before. She didn't run it as an inn, but I always saw the potential. You should have seen it before Mikel and Andre redid it. It was an eyesore. I have pictures," Jasmine said.

"I'd love to. Do you have any guests now?"

Jasmine nodded. The top of the staircase went in two different directions, winding around in a circle with several closed doors. Each door had a sign on it—*Seabreeze, Star fish, Anchor,* and *The Lighthouse Suite.* Jasmine turned left to the door marked *private.*

"Yes, two rooms are occupied at the moment. I have four up and running, then one for Zoey and me to share for now. The other room here isn't redone yet. Waiting on the money to do that. There are another couple large rooms downstairs that I eventually want to turn into my own living space for Zoey and me—away from the guest rooms, like a separate part of the house. But, for now, this will do." Jasmine opened the room where Zoey's little body was sprawled out in the crib, her tiny chest rising and falling. Her rosebud lips moved as if she was still suckling.

Mia's chest tightened. *I want that.* It was a shame she'd likely never have it. The ache in her heart intensified. "This is amazing, truly."

Jasmine looked down and shrugged. "I want to give my baby girl a safe home with stability. I figured this would be something that I would enjoy while also being able to keep her close to me."

"You are such a great mother." Mia smiled.

Jasmine's lips quirked up as she sat on the bed. "I never asked. Besides the studio, what do you do for work?"

"Won't we wake her up by talking in here?" Mia whispered, glancing over to Zoey one more time.

"She sleeps like the dead." Jasmine laughed lightly. "She'll be fine as long as we aren't too loud."

Mia sat across from Jasmine on the bed, setting the box between them. "I invested as a partner in an app that my friend from college and I developed. Turns out, it was a hit. Six months later, it was a bigger success than either of us imagined. I kept my shares and act as a silent partner now. I just get a check every month for taking that leap and investing my savings because I believed in my friend."

"Whoa. That's awesome. Which app, if you don't mind me asking?"

"Mig—it's an app that allows you to connect with other immigrants, attorneys, and resources specific to your area. People who come here and have nothing, or need jobs, or friends who understand their language and culture now have a way to connect." *It also told them in real time where ICE raids or road blocks are happening, along with listing people's rights in case they encountered an officer unlawfully asking for their papers.* But Mia wasn't ready to give that much away, so she kept that part to herself.

"That must be really helpful. Growing up, it was just me and my brothers. Mr. and Mrs. Stone were the only parental figures I had. They let me stay over a lot. I lived in poverty," Jasmine said, her eyes falling to a loose thread on her blue comforter. "But I can't imagine how hard it would be to be in a different country going through that, not speaking the language. It would feel so unsafe."

Mia nodded. That was exactly how she'd felt.

Jasmine continued, "I see stuff in the news about illegal immigrants being criminals and overpopulating our country."

Mia held her breath, unsure where Jasmine was going with this.

Jasmine shook her head. "But everyone I know originally from somewhere outside the United States are the hardest-working and kindest people I've ever met."

Relief flooded through Mia as she let go of the breath she'd been holding.

"I don't understand the laws, but I do see the farmers losing workers because no one else is willing to do the jobs that need to be done. Immigrants made this country what it is today. Unfortunately, it was built on the backs of black and brown people. We need to do better," Jasmine said, her voice surer.

"You're right. I have many friends who followed the law and it got them nowhere." *Myself included.* "It's a flawed system, and it needs to be fixed."

Jasmine nodded.

"What is your heritage, if you don't mind me asking?" Mia asked.

"My mother was your average European-American mix, and my father, I'm told, was Korean," Jasmine answered.

"Have you learned about the culture at all?" Mia asked.

Jasmine shook her head. "No . . . he was never a part of my life. Maybe someday I'll consider it."

Mia smiled. "Well, I brought you some things to clean out the energy in your home."

"I'll try anything once." Jasmine chuckled, something dark passing in her expression as she plastered on a smile too wide to be real.

Mia reached into the box, pulling out the clear stone. "This is a selenite tower crystal. It's great for bringing clarity and calm to your space, as well as luck and protection. Selenite is a high-vibration stone that helps clear energy, and open and activate your crown chakra." Mia pointed to her head. "For spiritual work."

Jasmine nodded. "Sounds like just what I need."

"This is a bundle of sage. We'll light the end until it begins to smoke and then we'll spread it throughout your room, and even over you to cleanse the air and clear the negative energy."

"Will it bother the baby?" Jasmine asked.

"Not at all. We won't do too much. Sage is scientifically proven to actually kill germs, so it's even good for the baby," Mia added.

Jasmine nodded. "Let's get started, then."

If only the sage could clear my attraction to Andre and give me the freedom to actually seek love to create a family. Now that would be some powerful magic.

Chapter 16

Andre

July turned into August. Joining Mia on her daily morning jog was the one guilty pleasure Andre allowed himself. Her shapely ass bounced just a few steps ahead of him. He'd let himself look, but not touch. *Well, not touch too much.* The little brushes of their hands, or when she playfully pushed him didn't count. Not even if he wished it could be more. When it came down to it, he liked spending time with her.

He tugged on her ponytail and sped up past her.

"Hey!" she screeched, hurrying her pace to shove him in the side, bumping her body against his.

He laughed. They didn't talk about themselves so much as they simply enjoyed the moments in each other's company. A friend. Yes, that was what Mia was. Just like Jasmine.

Except he'd never imagined Jasmine naked and writhing beneath him on the edge of pleasure.

* * *

Later that afternoon, Andre's phone rang from the desk in what would be Mia's office in a little less than six weeks.

"Hello?"

"Hey, Mr. Stone. This is Mike from down at Mackenzie

Lumber. I just wanted to let you know we've hit a snag in your delivery. It's gonna be delayed by a week."

"A week?" Andre clarified. He needed that lumber yesterday. This was going to throw their schedule behind. He had other clients waiting after this project with Mia. This was a disaster.

"Yes, sir. I'm sorry. There was a clerk error and the wrong wood was delivered. I apologize for any inconvenience."

Andre sighed. What else could he do?

"Fine. Thanks for letting me know." Andre hung up. His day had just gone south fast.

"Dre?" Tom asked, walking into the small room.

"Yeah?"

"We have a problem."

Andre rubbed his palm over his face. What now?

"You better come see."

Andre stood, following his right-hand man into the main part of the studio. As he walked through the building, he took note of all they'd accomplished. The list of what they had left to finish grew shorter every day. Mia was going to love it here. His stomach clenched at the thought of her face lighting up and her beautiful smile.

Tom laughed and Andre realized he hadn't been paying attention again. *Focus.* "Sorry. What did you say?"

"Flooring is all good, except this one section. I found some rot," Tom said, picking up a piece of the damaged wood. "It's a good thing after all that we tore up the floor."

Andre nodded. "Okay. You know what to do."

"Yeah, but that's the good news." Tom proceeded to show Andre the electrical mess he'd discovered in one of the walls—old wiring that should have been torn out ages ago and replaced. They were lucky it hadn't started a fire yet. Then Tom pointed out that one of the other guys had gone to mud and tape the ceiling in one of the future changing rooms, only to find water damage. A huge section would have to be redone.

As Tom listed off the setbacks, all Andre could do was grind his teeth together. This was a nightmare. He'd have to delay contracts and hope they'd wait for his business rather than seeking his competition. He and Mikel had been so close to reaching their goals, possibly hiring more men, but that hope had evaporated in the last fifteen minutes.

Andre returned to the office and started going over the amended plans for the next few days. *Then we'll paint the office and get Mia's proper desk placed in here.* A sturdy desk. Images of Mia spread out over said desk flashed in his mind.

Shit.

He reread the list. *Painting, then furniture.* A bed was a piece of furniture. The image of Mia almost naked in between her sheets with her hair sprawled out over the pillow flashed in his mind. He groaned. It was taking him twice as long because he couldn't stop thinking about Mia. *Get it together!* He could fall for her. But that was not a risk his heart could take.

Laughter and music filtered into the office. The noise grated on his last nerve. *Who the hell is joking around when we have so much work to do?*

Andre pushed his paperwork aside. It wasn't like he could get anything done anyways.

He walked down the hall to the main room where Tom was busy fitting in the new flooring. Upbeat salsa music was playing, and the woman who'd been on his mind all day every day for more than two months had conjured herself up. His chest tightened as he took a deep breath. Bently's arms wound around her as he spun and dipped her. The sight of her in his best friend's embrace made his veins burn with green venom. His hands itched to break them apart, even if only as an excuse to touch her. Mia's throaty laughter spilled out as Bently turned her.

God she's beautiful.

Andre leaned against the wall partition, he had no right to interrupt, because he had nothing to offer. He couldn't risk it.

"Mia, you're gonna make me beg, aren't you? You really know how to make a guy work for it." Bently bent on his knee as he held her hands. Andre's hands fisted.

Mia answered, "Oh, come on now. You like the chase—admit it."

Andre was used to Bently flirting with every woman. *But Mia is flirting back.* Andre stiffened, clenching his jaw.

Bently chuckled and smirked. "See, you know me so well already. Now let me take you out, or maybe we can stay in and *really* get to know each other."

The whine of a saw drowned out her answer as Andre stepped forward, unwilling to watch this play out any further.

"Bently!" Andre snapped.

"Ahhh!" Tom screamed as the saw shut off. Andre darted over to check on his employee, his attention focused and his body alert.

Tom clutched his hand to his chest, crimson blood trickling down his arm.

"Shit, Tom. Let me see," Andre said.

Tom unclenched his hand. Blood oozed from the deep slice across his finger, soaking his palm in red.

The music still played in the background as rigid tension

held Andre's body captive. Anxiety snaked around him. This could have ended a lot worse.

"Here. Keep pressure on it." Mia wrapped a few pieces of folded paper towels around his hand.

Tom squeezed the makeshift bandage over his injured finger.

Andre's anger simmered beneath the surface as she took over. How had this happened?

"Shut the music off!" Andre snapped.

All three sets of shocked eyes locked on him.

Mia stood and ran over to the speaker, silence blanketing the room.

Tom's face was twisted in pain.

"I'll take him to the ER. I was headed that way anyways," Bently offered.

Andre nodded. "That okay with you, Tom?"

"Yeah." Tom winced as Bently helped him to his feet.

Andre pulled out a card from his wallet and placed it in Tom's shirt pocket. "That's the information the hospital will need to bill me for the care. I'll call your wife if you want and have her meet you there?"

Tom shook his head. "No, I'll call her when I'm all patched up. Don't want her worrying and dragging the kids with her."

"Let me know if you need anything—and I mean *anything,* Tom," Andre said. Tom nodded as Bently ushered him out of the room.

Bently winked at Mia and said, "See you later."

Tom could have lost a hand. Andre could lose his workers' comp coverage and insurance would skyrocket. *I could lose my business.*

Andre turned his back, clenching his fists at his sides. The room was silent, Mia and Andre the only ones left on the property. They should have passed on this project. His lungs tightened, unable to draw a full breath as the gravity of the situation weighed heavily on his chest. Mia's scent saturated the air. Even now she was affecting him, and he hated her for it. Why did she hold so much power over him? It needed to stop.

"Are you okay?" Mia asked, her voice more timid than he was used to, which only served to enrage him further.

"No, I'm not. If you hadn't wanted to rip off this flooring to sprinkle your fairy dust, my guy wouldn't be on his way to the hospital at risk of losing his finger! The man's livelihood depends on his hands. We should have just sanded and poly'd the floors and forgot your voodoo," he growled. *Then we wouldn't have found the rot either.* Gah! It wasn't rational, but he wanted someone to take his anger out on for this.

"You're blaming me?" Her voice trembled as if she was using all her self-control to hold back.

"You had music blaring, were dancing around a work site while my guy was using a fucking saw. Who else's fault is it?"

"Maybe the man who walked into the room shouting and startling all of us," she fired back.

Fuck, she is right. His anger boiled, every nerve ending on alert as her spicy rose scent assaulted him, captivating his attention.

Her eyes held him hostage as she continued, "Or maybe it was human error and it's just an accident that happened. Your man will be fine. I'll make sure his family is cared for while he recovers."

His chest tightened as something foreign trickled through his veins. Walls shattered and broke at her offer, mixed with the sight of her perfect luscious curves as she stood her ground, unyielding. His lust overshadowed every other emotion. He was dying of thirst in a desert of isolation of his own making. Only she had the magic to quench this primal thirst.

"You're a distraction," he said, feeding her fire.

"Oh, so we're back to blaming me for everything?" She threw her hands up in the air. "Why do you feel the need to hate me so much? We were getting along. I thought we were friends." She sighed before her eyes locked with his and a small smile played on the corner of her lips.

"I can't be friends with you." It was the truth. Friends didn't want to fuck their friends.

"I see what this is about." She shook her head.

"Enlighten me." *Because I don't fucking know which way is up or down, east or west with you.*

"You're jealous Bently asked me out."

"That's ridiculous," he fired back.

"Is it? So, you won't mind when I invite him home . . . up to my bedroom?" Her eyes burned with the flames of a challenge as her lips curved into a knowing smile.

Something inside him snapped. His eyes darted to her lips only a second before his mouth was on hers. Mia's hands wrapped around his face as he pushed against her body so she could feel what she was doing to him. His rigid planes sought refuge in her soft curves. Pain mixed with the wildfire raging between them as she bit down on his lip. The electric charge that had been building since the moment he'd met her fueled an urgency. There was no time for thought—only action. He picked her up, Mia's legs wrapping around him tightly as he pressed her back to the wall. He moved, grinding his body against her, cursing the layers of clothing between them.

One hand cupped her breast as his mouth moved to her neck, biting and sucking as he marked her.

Her hands moved frantically to his waist while he set her on her feet long enough to unbutton his jeans and pull them down with his boxers. There was no time to take them all the way off. He slipped his fingers under the flowy pink skirt before ripping the small lace fabric of her panties off. She gasped. Her mouth continued its assault. Her lips moved, casting an erotic spell of greedy lust. An all-encompassing need to be inside her magnified and compounded. He took hold of her once more, overwhelming desire driving his actions. He slipped inside her hot wetness as delirium-inducing pleasure erupted down the base of his spine. He wasn't going to last long like this. It was too good. He moved his fingers to the pearl between her thighs as he rubbed and swirled. Leaning his head to her breast, he bit her nipple through the fabric as he thrust hard inside her.

She panted, her hot breath by his ear. "Yes. Oh, yes. Andre!"

Her words obliterated everything but his overwhelming urge to make her come. He moved faster, grunting each time he drove into her deeper. The scent of her arousal was potent and powerful. He locked eyes with her, adding a little more pressure to her clit as he slammed her body down on his. Her whimpers and cries and the string of Spanish coming from her mouth were like a bolt of pleasure straight to his cock.

"That's it. Come for me. I want to see that beautiful face when you become completely unhinged. Come for me, baby." He gave all his attention to that sweet, sensitive spot as her legs clamped around him like a vise.

"Dre!" Her mouth formed the perfect *O* as her pupils dilated. Tendrils of dark hair slipped over her face. His tongue swept inside her mouth, taking one more taste of her forbidden pleasure. Ecstasy gathered at his spine. The force was unstoppable as his cock throbbed and pulsed, emptying inside her.

Forehead against forehead, they stayed like that, her pressed against the wall, thighs wrapped around him. The panting of their breaths were the only sounds in the room as what they'd just done descended upon him like a tidal wave.

He set her down gently before pulling up his pants. Panic paralyzed him, taking away from the satiated bliss. *I didn't use a condom.* He didn't even carry them anymore.

Mia searched the ground before picking up the torn panties and balling them in her fist.

"I'm sorry." He ran a hand over his head. What else could he say after he'd acted on impulse and destroyed everything in a matter of minutes?

"It's okay. I can buy more," she said.

"We didn't use a condom."

"Oh," she said, obviously too caught up herself to realize their mistake. "I have an IUD, and I'm clean."

"I'm good too. I got checked after . . . There hasn't been anyone in more than a year," he said.

"Then we're all good." She smiled, taking a step closer to him.

"I'm not looking for a relationship."

Mia crossed her arms in front of her, her lips still swollen and pink from his kisses. His own mouth tingled where she'd bitten him. Fuck she was feisty. He wanted round two already.

"It's a good thing I'm not looking for one then." She furrowed her brow.

"This can't happen again," he clarified.

She sighed. "Fine. I'm not playing this game with you anymore."

"What game?" he snapped.

"The one where you pretend you don't want me and take out your sexual frustration on me because we have chemistry. It's just sex. I'm not asking for more. I can't have more." Her voice wavered on the last sentence.

Why did she believe that?

"I can't do *just sex* with a woman. I'm not that kind of guy." He stood straighter, holding on to the last shred of his pride.

"Oh yeah?" She turned to go, delivering her parting shot over her shoulder. "Because you just did."

Chapter 17

Andre

Turning left at the light, Andre drove down the road to The Shipwreck. His phone rang, and he answered using the Bluetooth option in his car.

"Hello?"

"Hey, Andre. It's Tom."

"Hey, buddy. How's the hand?" Andre asked, slowing as he approached the parking lot of the pub.

"Doc says it didn't go through the bone. Got some pain meds, and I'm all stitched up."

"That's great news." He cracked his neck as he pulled into a parking space. "I'll take care of the medical bill and send you your regular check until you recover enough to come back to work." Yes, it was generous, but he valued the man's work ethic and skill. It had been his fault Tom had gotten hurt in the first place. He'd make sure the man and his family were cared for, even if it put him in the red.

"You don't have to do that—"

"I insist, Tom. You're a valued member of our crew," Andre argued.

"Thank you, sir. It's just that Miss Garcia stopped by the hospital and gave me a check already. I wouldn't have taken it, but she handed it to my wife and insisted she'd cleared it with you. I wish I didn't need it, but I'm the only one bringing in money in my family."

Mia had visited his employee? She'd paid him? She had said she would.

"Let me know if it's not enough, or if you need anything else," Andre said.

"I will. And I'll be back to work as soon as the doctor clears me. I want to pay her back. I know I'm leaving you in the lurch." Tom's voice lowered as if he were ashamed. There was nothing shameful about doing what you needed to do to support your family and put food in your kids' mouths.

"I know you'll be back at it in no time. You have a good night with your family."

"You too," Tom said before ending the call.

Andre sighed, a mixture of emotions battering his rib cage. He'd fought with Mia and blamed her for Tom's injury, then he'd fucked her before picking yet another fight with her. He was an asshole. Why was everything falling apart, slipping through his hands like quicksand?

What had he done? He'd crossed lines that could never be uncrossed. It was reckless and stupid, not even using a condom. He hadn't asked her if she wanted it—he'd acted like an animal. Though she had too. He smiled, touching the tender flesh of his bottom lip that was still sore from her bite.

Maybe now that she was out of his system, he would be able to carry on and not react so strongly to her.

Andre climbed from the truck and headed into the pub to meet Bently and Mikel. He nodded to Mason, the guy who worked security most evenings.

"Hey, buddy. Nice night."

One side of Mason's scarred face turned up into a smile. "Sure is."

Opening the door, Andre entered the blue-lit room. The giant fish tanks built into the walls on either side danced water shadows across the dance floor.

Bently was already seated at the bar with Mikel, making him the last to arrive.

"Look what the cat dragged in," Mikel said, before taking a drink of his soda.

He had to hand it to the man, staying sober while having temptation thrown in his face all the time. Andre didn't know if he'd be able to abstain, and yesterday evening with Mia was proof of his lack of self-control.

"What are you two troublemakers up to tonight?" Andre asked, taking a seat next to Bently.

"Bent is having a bit of woman troubles," Mikel supplied.

Andre exaggerated his shocked expression. "The myth, the legend—the man-whore of Shattered Cove is having . . . woman troubles?"

Bently punched his arm hard enough to leave a bruise. "It's not like this guy could help. He's been a fucking priest for the last year, unless you hooked up with that blonde a while back?"

Andre shook his head. "Nah. I don't have it in me to take the kind of risks you do." *Except with Mia apparently.*

"What risks? My heart isn't ever involved. I think you might be defective. You are the only man I've ever known to always get his heart involved when he uses his dick. Don't you know they're separate organs?" Bently chuckled and took another swig of his beer.

"I meant risks like herpes, you dumb fuck." Andre smacked his friend's back.

"What can I get you, Dre?" Charli asked.

"I think I need the hard stuff tonight," Andre answered.

"It's probably the only thing that gets hard for you anymore." Bently and Mikel burst out laughing.

He could end all of this teasing with the fact that he had gotten laid just yesterday, but then his friends would ask too many questions.

"Alright, lay off Dre. This is about you, bro. And how you've been chasing a woman who won't give you the time of day," Mikel said.

"What? Your charms aren't working on someone for once?" Andre smirked.

"They seem to have the opposite effect on her actually," Bently grumbled.

Does he mean Mia? The tiny hairs on the back of Andre's neck stood on end. The air around him buzzed with an electric current as his senses became hyper-aware. He turned around, catching sight of her brown eyes. His chest tightened as he struggled to draw a breath.

Mia looked away from him as she walked towards the bar. She had on a bright yellow dress that stopped a few inches above her knee. Her coffee hair spilled loosely over her shoulders as she brushed a stray lock from her face.

"You know what they say though—try, try again," Bently said. "I think I'll practice a little more with Mia." He laughed as Mia approached them with a hesitant smile directed at his buddy.

Dread and pain coursed through Andre, jealousy rearing its ugly head. He still couldn't believe they'd had sex. Explosive, world-shaking sex. Mia had to be the one Bently was talking about. *I'm so fucked.*

"Hey, baby," Bently said, standing to give Mia a hug. Andre clenched his fists and grabbed the glass Charli had placed in front of him at some point, savoring the burn of the alcohol as he downed it in one shot.

"Another." He waved to Charli.

"Sorry I'm late," Mia said.

"You're right on time, and my, you look delicious."

Andre wasn't facing them, but he would bet his business Bently was flashing Mia his best smile complete with eye-fucking. This shouldn't bother him as much as it did.

Mia laughed. "Is he always this much?"

Mikel answered her, "Bently never changes. His ego is bigger than anyone else I know."

"That's not all that's big," Bently said.

Charli tugged at the glass in Andre's hand. He'd been gripping it like a vise as she studied him curiously. She filled it with more amber liquor.

"Thanks," he said, taking another drink as soon as she'd finished. Maybe he could drown the turmoil wreaking havoc in his chest with the alcohol.

"Don't mind our rude friend. He's just cranky because he hasn't gotten laid in a loooong time," Bently joked, as Andre turned around to face them.

Mia's eyes darted from him to the dance floor, her cheeks glowing with a slight blush as her finger traced the light purple bruise on her neck where he'd marked her. She'd done her best to cover it with makeup, erase him. Too bad he couldn't forget her.

"That's okay. How about a dance?" she asked Bently.

He hooked his arm around her waist and led her towards the other couples on the dance floor.

"You okay, man?" Mikel asked.

"Just peachy."

"You worried about what happened to Tom?" Mikel took another sip of his drink.

"Yeah, he's gonna pull through though," Andre answered his friend as Bently pulled Mia close, wiggling his hips and spinning her around. She laughed. His hands roamed dangerously low, landing just above her ass. *The same ass I had in my hands as I came inside her little more than twenty-four hours ago.*

Mikel chuckled, but he'd missed whatever he'd said. Andre was too preoccupied by Bently and Mia. The woman he wanted. Fuck, he did want her. Again, and again.

"I'm gonna head home. It's my turn to put the kids to bed while Remy has some alone time," Mikel said, throwing some bills onto the bar top.

"See you later." Andre nodded, not taking his eyes from Mia.

Mikel leaned in and spoke close to his ear. "You know he brought her here to rile you up, right?"

"What?"

Mikel nodded towards the dance floor. "He's got it bad for some other girl who won't give him the time of day. He said he's lost all interest in other women. The only reason he invited Mia was to get your stubborn ass back into enjoying life."

Bently didn't want Mia? "What the hell does Mia have to do with that?"

"Dude, you really are in denial. The tension between you two is white-hot."

"That's why we fight like cats and dogs?"

Mikel shook his head and chuckled. "Sometimes the best

fucking comes after all that fighting. All that passion bottled up."

If only Mikel knew how right he was. "I don't need to hear that shit about my sister."

Mikel shrugged. "I'm not saying Bent won't take advantage of your situation. You know how he is. It's now or never." His friend walked away, leaving him alone at the bar to stew in the anger and jealousy radiating through every cell of his body.

Mia's head rested on Bently's shoulder as they moved to a slow dance. Did she fit Bently's body as perfectly as she'd felt against his?

Andre gulped the rest of his drink and got to his feet. His heart raced the closer he got. He tapped on Bently's shoulder.

"Mind if I cut in?"

Bently smirked like he'd won the biggest prize at the fair. "About damn time."

Mia looked between the two men, obviously as in the dark about this setup as he had been.

"I gotta get going anyways. You'll make sure she gets back to her car safe?" Bently asked.

"Of course." Andre wrapped his arms around Mia as they started to dance.

"What is this?" she asked, straight to the point.

"Did you know I was going to be here?"

She shook her head. "I agreed to meet Bently for a drink. I figured it would just be us. He's been asking me for a while."

"It really was just sex to you?" he asked, emotion clogging his throat. What answer did he want from her?

"Yes." Her voice rose an octave higher with her answer.

"Do you still want that?"

She pulled back to look him in the eyes. "I've made it no

secret that I'm attracted to you. I meant it when I said I can't do a relationship right now. It will just be sex, nothing more."

"Then I just have one more question for you." He nearly growled his words as his cock throbbed with the fantasies playing out in his head that could now come to fruition.

"What?" Her voice came out breathy as she slid her hands over his chest.

"Your place, or mine?"

Chapter 18

Andre

A ndre held Mia's hand as they rushed through the alley in the darkness.

"Do you always walk through here at night?" Shattered Cove was a safe town, but things still happened.

"No, it was just such a beautiful night, so I left my car at the studio." After a moment of silence, she laughed. "I can't believe stone-cold Andre is actually going through with this."

He stopped abruptly, pulling her close enough to taste her cinnamon breath on his lips. "I couldn't resist you." Pawing her ass, he pulled her tightly against him.

She let loose the tiniest of moans and his cock twitched against his pants in anticipation of the fun ahead. It was going to be a long night. "Little witch?"

"Me?" she asked, her voice molten.

He nodded, his nose brushing hers in the darkness. Her face glowed in the moonlight. The lunar sphere glinted off the broken glass in the otherwise black alley.

"I'm gonna make you come on my mouth."

She licked her lips as a breathy sigh left her. Her thighs clenched against his.

"How many times have you ever come in one day?" he

asked, enjoying the torturous foreplay with words. There was no need to rush this time—they had all night.

"Just one."

"Then I can't wait to show you what it's like to fuck a real man." He kissed her jaw as she tilted her head to grant him better access. He ran his finger over the makeup covering the bruise on her skin. "You tried to hide this?"

"Yes," she admitted.

"Don't ever do that again," he said, slipping into the commanding role that came so naturally to him.

"If I do, will you punish me?" she asked, her eyes wild with lust.

His heart rate increased as her words shot arrows of desire through his chest. Damn if this woman wasn't perfect enough. That was the hottest thing he'd ever heard. "You'd like that, wouldn't you?"

She bit her lip and looked him confidently in the eyes. "Yes, but I should warn you—I'm a stubborn woman, so it may take a lot of punishment to teach me a lesson."

Dead. He was gone. All the blood rushed to his cock. He needed to have her. *Right fucking now.*

His mouth crashed onto hers as his tongue invaded Mia's mouth, seeking to conquer just a piece of the control she'd stolen away from him. She moaned, leaning into him, surrendering. He pulled back to drink her in. The moon highlighted her glossy swollen lips and lust-filled eyes. He couldn't wait any longer.

Mia's gaze widened, and her shoulders tensed under his grip. Before he could utter another word, cold sharp metal pressed against his neck.

"Back up slowly or I'll cut your throat," a malicious voice said.

Every muscle in his body went rigid. Fear coated Mia's expression. She trembled. He backed away from her, following instructions, hands held up.

"What do you want?" Andre asked, assessing the situation. Every muscle in his body went rigid, his senses on high alert. He was ready to fight, to protect his woman. *My woman?*

"Your wallet is a good start." Rough hands reached into his back pocket, pulling out his billfold.

"Sure, man. Take it and leave us alone."

The guy chuckled. He sounded young, like a teenager.

"Get her jewelry," the one with the knife said as a dark figure moved from behind the shadows. An accomplice's footsteps crunched on broken glass.

"I didn't sign up for this, man. W-what are you doing?" a kid in a red sweatshirt, no more than five and a half feet tall, asked timidly, his eyes darting around nervously.

"Just shut up and do what I said or your pretty sister is next," knife guy growled at the shaky kid.

The kid walked over to Mia and tried to unclasp her necklace. Mia shifted, turning her face slightly away. Andre's self-control was fraying at the edges, about to snap. He wanted to fight back. But he had to protect Mia. They just needed to give these guys what they wanted and they would leave them alone. That was the safest option.

Mia moved her shaking hands behind her body, not making a sound.

"I'm sorry," the kid said, struggling with the clasp in the dark.

"Just rip it off!" the first guy yelled as the knife pressed harder into Andre's neck.

Andre's body was too fueled on adrenaline to do more than register the pain.

Knife-guy reached to the side of Andre and yanked on the chain as Mia winced.

"Don't you fucking touch her!" Andre snapped.

The knife ground tighter against his throat. Andre winched his face towards the night sky. The blade serrated into his skin.

His attacker chuckled. "I can take whatever I want from her and there isn't a damn thing you could do about it. I'm the one with the power here, not you."

Fuck. He was right. Andre was powerless with the weapon pressed to his throat. Rage burned him from the inside out like hellfire sent straight from Hades himself. His hands itched with helplessness. There was no way he'd let this motherfucker lay a finger on Mia. *Over my dead body.*

"You got what you wanted. Now leave us alone," Mia said, her voice steadier than her trembling body.

The knife loosened enough for him to look down at her.

"I want that ring you're hiding behind your back too," his attacker sneered.

"It's not worth much. Please, it—it was my mother's." Her voice sounded so small. *Damn it, Mia. Just give them the ring.*

"Hand it over or I'll cut it off."

Mia's gaze hardened as she twisted the gold band from her finger and placed it in the timid kid's hand.

"Now count to one hundred and don't turn around until then. If you do, I'm gonna pay a little visit to the address from this wallet and make you regret the day you were born. And don't think I can't find out where you live, dirty whore," he threatened Mia.

The knife disappeared from Andre's aching neck as the sound of running footsteps echoed in the dark alley.

She sighed, taking two shaky steps forward before collapsing against his chest, as his arms went out instinctively to hold her.

"Are you hurt?" He carefully caressed her face and her neck as if he could tell through touch alone. Concern laced around him, constricting his airway as her eyes grew glassy.

"Just my pride . . . and my mother's ring." She sniffled.

"Let's go. We need to get somewhere safe and then call Bently," Andre said, taking her hand and hurrying the rest of the way out of the alley. They emerged in the busy Main Street under the lights, where several pedestrians milled about.

"Let's just forget this ever happened. Don't call Bently," she said, and he stopped in his tracks, doing a double take.

"We were just robbed by knifepoint," he said, touching his neck before examining the red blood on his fingers. *Is she in shock?*

Mia looked down. "I know. If you want to go, that's fine, but please leave me out of it."

"But you were there. You were assaulted too, Mia. You saw the one with the knife's face. I didn't. The fucker has my license. He knows where I live." How could the same woman who'd held it together when their lives were being threatened fall to pieces at a simple task of reporting the crime to the police? *What if Mia had walked through here alone?*

Tears fell down her cheeks as her broken expression morphed into terror. "I know. Please, Andre, leave me out of this. If Bently comes and asks me, I'm going to say nothing."

Surely he had stepped into an alternate reality.

"Why?"

She shook her head. "I can't . . ."

If nothing else about the situation made sense, the fear in her eyes was real.

"Let's get you home," he said, but his mind spun.

She'd seemed afraid to report the guy who'd shoved her over the cliff too. A pattern was forming. Andre's stomach sunk. Somewhere, sometime, something had happened to Mia. Something *terrible*.

Chapter 19

Mia's Letter

*F*or the first couple years after we were denied asylum, my mother checked in yearly with Immigration and Customs Enforcement as I've said. I focused on my degree while working full-time at several different jobs. I was so determined to graduate and be able to give my mother a life with less stress about income.

My friend Carmen is a programmer. During my last semester in college, we worked together to develop an app to help immigrants find resources and connect with others in their location for support.

I watched as families were ripped apart. Our elderly neighbor had served in the military for twenty-five years before he lost a leg while putting his life on the line in service of the very country that deported him.

I've been yelled at, propositioned, and assaulted all because of where I was born or the color of my skin—none of which I could control. Judged not for my heart, but my skin and heritage. I know you can understand what that is like.

To be accepted into DACA (Deferred Action for Childhood Arrivals) you cannot have a criminal record. I thought this was common knowledge, but as the protests increased and immigration became the issue all over the news cycles, I heard them spreading lies on national television. They called us murderers, rapists, and criminals.

I lived in fear of leaving the house. Would I be stopped and asked *for my papers? At least I was protected by DACA, but would the ICE officers obey the law and let me go? Would they detain me for however long they wished or deport me?*

We are just like you. We are good, hardworking people trying to live a safe and better life for ourselves and our families. Some flee violence, others poverty, or some seek a better opportunity. Isn't that what your founding fathers said this country was for? "Give me your tired, your poor, your huddled masses yearning to breathe free" is carved on your Statue of Liberty.

During this time, my mother still had to work, and she didn't have papers. She'd take the bus rather than risk driving herself. When they started raiding buses, she began walking if I was at school and couldn't drive her.

Each year, we received a letter from the cartel describing in detail what they were going to do to us. How they would dismember and torture us. They kept a detailed list of all the men who would rape us. They knew where we lived. That's the thing about fear—when you live with it like a roommate every day of your life, it becomes the bar for what's normal. You get used to it. And once you get comfortable, that's when the real terror starts.

Executive orders were passed under the new administration by the same president who claimed he'd only deport criminals. My mother went for her usual yearly check-in with ICE, and as I waited for her to come out, I got a call to say my friend's app had taken off and she'd been offered a large sum of money by another company who wanted to join our partnership. I was so excited to tell Mamá the news. To tell her she didn't have to work so hard anymore. I could take care of her and she could rest and relax and volunteer like she'd wanted but never had time to do.

When she walked out of the building, my glee quickly faded, morphing into a sick feeling that twisted in my gut. Her face was ashen, drained of life as she approached the car.

I asked her what happened and then, with her next words, she tore out my heart.

"I'm being deported, mija. *I have thirty days."*

I held the tears in as a fierce determination overtook everything. "No, you won't, Mamá. This can't be right. I'll fix this. Don't you worry," I promised her.

I visited our senators, wrote to those in power in our state. I paid for a handful of lawyers with what money I'd saved. I petitioned and did everything else I could, but it wasn't enough.

The last day my mother was in the U.S., I went over all our possibilities. Her life was at stake, and the only people who could protect us turned their faces away from us, pretending people like us were not the very lifeblood of this country. The new partnership with the app was still pending, and the funds were not accessible or I'd have paid the cartel off. I'd have given everything so that my mother would be safe.

I borrowed from friends to pay a coyote to return my mother as soon as she landed in Mexico. She packed light, because she'd be returning. I knew the journey would be hard on her. She was not as young as she'd been the first time we'd crossed. I pleaded with her to let me go with her, but she refused.

She gave me her wedding ring and told me to keep it because it carried the love that my father had for her, and they in turn had for me. That someday, it would help me find my love. I remember the way she smelled—like wild rose with a hint of lemon cleaner.

I think in my heart I knew she was saying goodbye, but my mind wouldn't believe it. She was just preparing me for the worst, while hoping for the best.

I hugged her as tightly as I could. "The coyote will find you when you land—his name is Javier. I'll see you at the border in a few days." I kissed her cheek.

She smiled, not bothering to wipe the tears streaming down her face.

"*I love you, mija. I just want you to live a life that makes you happy and keeps you safe. I'm so proud of you.*"

She kissed my forehead and gave me one final hug before she walked away. She left on a plane, taking her back to the land in which she was born—a place I barely remembered.

That was the last time I saw my mother alive.

Chapter 20

Mia

Stretching out her leg, Mia arched her back into pigeon pose. She exhaled, focusing on her breath. Her muscles were still a little sore. *Because of Andre.* And the most explosive sex she'd ever had. She bit back the smile. Shaking her head in an attempt to refocus her thoughts, she glided forward into upward dog and then down to plank. A delicious heat stirred in her belly, but she'd blame it on the planks and not the image flashing in her mind of the intense desire in his eyes. There had been something so primal about the way he'd taken her like that. She'd never connected that way with any of her lovers before. *Too bad the shadow that followed her all her life had to go and ruin it so soon.* Would he go to the police? Anxiety gripped her chest, constricting her airway.

Ping!

Mia shot a quick glance at her upside-down phone out of habit. The message could wait.

She eased onto her back as she relaxed and stretched out her sore muscles. Her neck ached from having her necklace ripped from her the night before. Bending her knees to her chest, she rocked side to side. Spreading her arms out, she straightened into her final pose of rest for a few minutes as she filled her belly with air. Beads of sweat trickled down her forehead as she let herself drift into her safe place.

She could have taken all that had happened in her life and chosen to be bitter and stay closed off from people in her life like Andre seemed to. But she owed her parents more. They didn't die so that she could become a shell. Mia was going to do exactly as they wanted and be happy. She'd help others too. That was how she'd live in their legacy.

Ping!

She exhaled and sat up, reaching for her phone.

Mateo: *Buenos días, beautiful! My flight gets in next Thursday morning at 9 and I can stay until 4. I have to drive to Boston after that for some meetings.*

Mia: *I guess we have quite a lot to do in such little time. Can't wait to see you! I miss you.*

She plugged in her cell by the bed and rolled up her mat before heading to take a shower.

A little while later, Mia was dressed in a pair of shorts and a white V-neck as she brushed out her long, wet hair. Knocking sounded from the first floor. She jogged down the stairs and opened the door.

"Andre." She searched for any sign he'd brought Bently or another policeman. Only green grass and trees stood behind him. She let out a sigh of relief.

"Can we talk?" he asked.

"Sure." Mia opened the door, allowing him access.

They walked over to the kitchen island and he took a seat.

"I was just going to make some coffee. Do you want some?" she asked.

Please don't be here about the mugging.

"No, I, uh … I just wanted to talk about the other night."

Shit. Option number two it is, then—distracting with flirtation.

"Well, we could go upstairs and you could show me. You made a lot of promises." She smiled, hoping he'd take the bait and not bring up the mugging again.

His eyes darkened as he stared at her protruding nipples. She had no plans of leaving the house, so she'd gone without a bra.

He swallowed. "Not about that. About the robbery."

"I told you—I just want to forget it ever happened."

"Is there a reason why you don't want to go to the cops and report it?"

She met his gaze as her whole body flushed with heat. Did he know?

Should I just tell him?

"They were kids. I'm worried about the younger one. It was obvious he did it under duress. The one with the knife threatened his sister." It was true.

"All the more reason to talk to Bently," he argued.

She'd walked right into that one. "Andre, you have every right to report it if you haven't already. I am choosing not to. It's too . . . risky."

His expression softened as he stood and walked over to her. He caressed her cheek softly. "Are you worried he'll come back and hurt you?"

Was she? He didn't have her information, but if he sat outside Andre's house, the maniac would be sure to see her. It didn't matter. He was the least of her worries.

"Please don't ask me to do this. I just can't." She leaned into his hand, drinking in the physical contact. It was a shame this would be all that would ever happen between them. She had promises to keep.

"I have a friend who works with homeless teens and runs a program for youth in the city. I'll visit him and see if he knows anyone that fits the bill. I can ask if he has any idea who the younger one could be. Maybe we can help each other. He gives up the guy, and you don't have to have any part in it."

"You'd do that?" *For me?*

Andre nodded.

"What is the name of this place?"

Maybe the kids would benefit from a yoga and mindfulness class.

"Hope Facility. My friend Aaron runs it."

She nodded.

His hand traced the edge of her chin as he leaned in to brush his lips softly against hers. A rush of sensations splintered through her with the contact. She brought her arms around his neck, and he deepened the kiss. Opening her mouth, she tasted him with her tongue. Gripping the back of his neck, she pulled him closer. She'd enjoy this explosive chemistry between them while it lasted. She wanted more—needed him.

"I want you, right now." She hoped he could sense her impatience.

His hands moved down her shoulders, slipping farther to her hips as he lifted the hem of her shirt over her head. He broke the kiss to free her top, and she shivered as the cool air met her hard nipples. Her core throbbed with overpowering need. What was this man doing to her?

His eyes glazed over as he licked his lips, admiring her breasts. Her nipples ached in anticipation. Andre leaned down, sucking one into his mouth.

She gasped and moaned. The heat of his tongue against

the sensitive flesh was almost enough to make her come on the spot. One of his hands cupped the other breast as his teeth raked over the hard nub. Fire tingled from the base of her neck and spread throughout her body, until every cell was aflame with unbridled yearning. "Andre, I need you."

He pulled away, breaking the contact. "And you're going to have me. But first, I believe I promised to make you come on my tongue."

Damn. If her panties weren't already soaked, they were now.

He reached for the button on her shorts and pulled them off, letting them drop to the floor. Her white lace panties didn't last much longer, and then she was completely bare—standing in front of him with nothing but hazy lust intoxicating her senses.

"You're fucking perfect." Andre picked her up before setting her on the granite countertop. The frigid surface only registered for a moment as he spread her thighs and pulled her core to the edge. Fire and ice ravaged her body at once as his head dipped lower and his tongue lapped between her slick folds.

The sight of his head bobbing between her legs as his tongue lashed greedily at her pussy created a swirling vortex of pleasure. Until nothing else in the world existed except her euphoria. He devoured her as her body trembled, growing closer to her release.

He groaned as if this too was bringing him satisfaction. "You taste just like I thought you would. Sweet and spicy." He dove back in, sucking her clit into his mouth as she screamed.

The orgasm took hold as she arched her back, grabbing his head and pulling him closer. His expert mouth sucked, swirled, and raked. The tormenting pleasure left her with a hollow ache.

"I need you inside me. Please," she begged, coming down from her high.

He kissed a trail up her thigh, over her soft belly, stopping to lave at her breasts. "You'll have to wait, beautiful. I promised you more orgasms, and by my count, that's just the first. I'm gonna take my time and savor each one." He kissed her mouth, her essence still on his tongue. The heady aroma of her own arousal was mixed with his clean wood musk.

"I don't think you understand. I *need* you. Please? I'll do anything you want—just please get inside me," she begged in a wanton haze of sex-induced delirium.

He smirked against her mouth. "I promise to take you up on that, but I have another climax to deliver first. I have this client who's a real pain in my ass. I'm hoping that a few orgasms will put her in a better mood."

Mia laughed. "Your boss, huh?"

He sucked her bottom lip into his mouth as his fingers entered her. She gasped as he moved them in and out as his other hand played with her sensitive clit.

"*Dios*, Dre!"

"That's it, baby. Let me hear you."

Mia let go, pleasure penetrating her ability to do anything other than experience the moment. She didn't hold back as she screamed and moaned. He brought her to orgasm again in one long climax. She sat up, her nails digging into his back, as if he could keep her tethered to earth as her soul was shattered by his plundering fingers. He sucked the side of her breast, the pain sharpening the debilitating euphoria. Pleasure saturated every nerve ending as she was blanketed in warmth. Her muscles grew limp. His strong arms held her, picking her up. She laid her head against his warm, hard chest as he carried her towards her bedroom.

He gently set her on the soft comforter before he stripped his shirt off. Mia was dazed with satiated bliss. His brown muscles were defined and rigid. He bent to slip his boots off before he pulled his tan Carhartts down. His cock sprang free, glistening with proof of his own desire.

The look in his eyes was hungry. All his lust was aimed at her, making her feel powerful for the first time in her life. Tears burned her eyes, and she blinked them away. *This is just sex. That's all he wants. That's all I can have.*

He removed a foil wrapper out of his pocket before he climbed on top of her.

She reached out her open palm. "Let me?"

Andre handed her the condom. She ripped it open, sliding her hand over his rock-hard cock as he hissed.

"Put it on," he demanded as if he was in pain.

She pinched the end and rolled it over him, pumping her hand up and down a few times before he growled and grabbed her, intertwining his fingers with hers. He pinned them above her head as he slid inside in one hard thrust. She closed her eyes, relishing the connection. Her inner muscles clenched, needing him to move. Andre's forehead touched hers, each breath matching her own as he pumped slowly in and out of her. The grip of his hands on hers, pinning her to the bed, tightened as if he was fighting his self-control to go slow. She wrapped her legs around him, pulling him closer.

There was no other sound in the room except their labored panting and the slap of flesh against flesh as Andre showed her what it was to . . . whatever this was. She'd never fucked like this before. What was it called when it was more than sex? When emotion twisted and tangled, the soul merging with the physical? *It's just amazing sex. It can never be more.*

"Harder." She opened her eyes as he lifted his head to stare at her. His forehead creased with his own impending pleasure.

He released her hands, and she immediately gripped his shoulders and kissed him. He sat up, spreading her legs apart on either side of him as he drove into her. She stretched her thighs as wide as they would go, allowing him deeper access.

"Give it to me. Yes. Dre!"

"Come with me." His voice was needy and desperate with passion.

She was propelled over the edge into oblivion. Pleasure gathered, tingling, shooting through her as he cried out with her. The orgasm rolled, blasting Mia like a tidal wave, potent and powerful. She raked her hands over his shoulders, and he lowered himself on her as if he too had never felt anything so raw and complete in his life.

After a few moments, he kissed her gently and slid out. She immediately missed the connection.

He rolled over and extended his arm for her to lie on. Who would have known Andre liked to snuggle?

"That was . . ." She searched for the right words to describe the elation and utter devastation she felt, knowing she'd probably never have this with another man—knowing this wouldn't last.

"Perfection." He smiled.

She lay in a limbless puddle, naked in his warm arms, savoring the moment. Life was just a culmination of moments after all. She was beginning to care a lot more for Andre than she could afford to. Maybe they could just remain good friends after all was said and done.

Ping! Her phone chimed, no doubt with a reply from Mateo. A reminder of why all of this couldn't last.

Even if Andre somehow wanted this to be more someday, Mia was not free to make that choice. She had promises of her own she needed to fulfill. And none of those involved Andre Stone.

Chapter 21

Andre

After pulling into an empty parking spot, Andre cut the ignition and climbed out of the truck. His steps had felt lighter this past week. Everything was back on track at the jobsite, and almost every night he ended up at Mia's door—and then usually her bed. It was the best sex of his life.

He entered through the double doors of the Hope Facility. Passing the lobby, he walked into the large room used for speakers and group meetings. A few clusters of teenagers were gathered in the area, laughing and talking. Andre searched their faces for any sign of the scared accomplice who'd been with their assailant in the alley.

"Dre."

Andre turned as Aaron's smiling face greeted him. "My man. How are you?"

Aaron nodded and reached out one of his long arms to slap hands with him. "Not bad, my friend. You?" Aaron asked.

Andre returned the gesture, ending it with a fist bump. He surveyed the room of mostly disinterested teens. "Is there somewhere private we can talk?"

Aaron's brow furrowed and he crossed his arms. "Sure. Let's go to my office."

They walked along a hallway and stepped into a room that Andre had renovated himself. He'd had a big hand in helping Aaron's dreams become a reality in this place. The centerpiece was a large cherry desk. Pictures of Aaron playing pro ball accented the blue walls, along with his certifications of philanthropy and his degree in social work and psychology. Locked file cabinets lined one side, no doubt filled with the hundreds of names and related documents on each child and teenager who came through the doors needing a refuge.

Aaron took a seat behind his desk and motioned for Dre to sit across from him. "What's on your mind?" Aaron asked as the chair squeaked.

"My—" *Shit, I almost said girlfriend.* "My friend and I got mugged last week."

Aaron sat up straighter. "I'm sorry, man. You guys okay?"

"Yeah. Um, I'm here because the younger kid didn't seem to want to be a part of it, and the piece of shit who held a knife to my throat threatened his sister. I don't know. I figured it was worth mentioning to see if you've heard anything. I can describe the kid I saw, but not the one with the knife."

Aaron let out a whistle. "What about your friend? Did they see the other guy's face?"

Andre drew in a deep breath. "She wants to stay out of it."

Aaron raised his eyebrows. "She?"

"Oh, for fuck's sake. I don't need to hear it from you too. Did you miss the part about her just being a *friend?*"

Aaron smirked. "All right. Well, I have picked up on some whispers about some low-level gang activity happening in the outskirts of the city, specifically Shattered Cove. More like a wannabe gang, if you will. Some of the kids mentioned having run into an older teen, maybe early twenties. Guy has ties to a bigger dealer. Could be him—maybe not. You and your . . . *friend* should be careful."

A gang? In Shattered Cove? Andre shook his head. "I can't believe it. This is the most family-friendly town I know."

"Drug dealers come in from out of state, get the kids hooked, then turn them into dealers themselves. Most of these kids are dealing with so much pain, trouble at home—hell, you remember what it was like being a teenager. So many hormones, needing to impress, not fitting in. Opioids are an epidemic, and a lot of the population get their first fix from their doctor. They lead a completely normal life, then they get an injury, and bam. They're addicted."

Andre had watched Mikel go through his struggles with addiction. "Wish there was something more I could do."

"Why don't you give me a description of this kid you saw and I'll try to identify if I know him? I can ask around."

Andre nodded.

After giving his friend the details, he said goodbye and headed back to his truck. He'd left work a couple of hours early to make this trip to Aaron's and be back to surprise Mia with dinner. He'd cook this time. They'd need sustenance for the hours he planned on spending finding new ways to make her come. His body buzzed with anticipation—she was the one person who could make him feel alive. The one person who didn't drill him about his personal life. Mia lived in the moment, and he wanted more of them.

Pulling into his driveway, his brow furrowed. An expensive-looking BMW was parked in front of Mia's. He grabbed his lunchbox and headed inside to shower off the sweat and sawdust from his long hours at work.

Did Mia have a friend visiting? An uncomfortable knot

formed in his gut as he stripped his clothing and climbed in the shower. The hot water cleansed his skin, but he couldn't shake the unease that weighed on his shoulders.

After shutting off the spray, he grabbed his towel and dried off. Tying it around his waist, he peered out the window. Her bedroom curtains were closed. He could text her and ask her if he could come over, but he didn't even have her phone number. Mikel had it though. However, if she had company, then maybe he should give her space. It wasn't like they were dating. Panic struck him. Was she still seeing other people?

He got dressed and went down to the kitchen to start the pasta. As the water heated, he searched out the window for any sign of Mia. Movement in the kitchen caught his attention—Mia and some tall stranger.

A man was in Mia's house.

Jealousy burned his veins as he clenched his fists. He should have known better.

"Fuck!"

He ran a hand over his head as he moved to the front of the house, eyes locked on her door as it opened. A man with tan skin and dark hair followed her outside as they walked towards his car. Andre drew in rapid breaths as his chest constricted. Mia was smiling as the man swept her up in a hug and she gave him a peck on the lips.

Did she sleep with him? Why else would he be there?

Mia had money, and by the looks of it, so did this guy. Did Mia want that? Sure, Andre did just fine, but he wasn't the BMW-owning, suit-wearing type. He was a blue-collar man through and through. Mia was cheating on him. No. They weren't dating. She'd made that clear. They'd agreed. So why did this feel like his heart was being ripped out of his chest? It hadn't felt this intense even when Tiffany had confessed.

The water sizzled from where it spilled over, boiling. Andre went to the kitchen and turned off the stove. He wasn't hungry anymore. He was pissed. He grabbed the bottle of whiskey from the cupboard and filled himself a glass. He threw back the amber liquid until it didn't burn anymore.

Hours went by. The clock on the wall ticked loudly as if mocking him. Should he confront her? Should he just end this and forget it had ever happened? *Yeah, right.* Like that was possible. Now he knew what he would be missing. Maybe it was just a friend. *A friend she kissed on the mouth.* It didn't seem like a lover's kiss though.

He shook his head, the room mildly spinning. He was going to go crazy if he sat here stewing over every little possibility. He stood, setting his empty glass on the side table. He needed to get this over with.

He trudged to her door, breathing in the humid night air. He cleared his throat and rang her bell.

Her soft footsteps came closer as he straightened his shoulders. Her figure, blurred by the glass door, still managed to make his lungs hitch.

Mia opened the door, a big grin on her face. Her tanned body was wrapped in a pink silk robe. His hands itched to grab her, to make her forget any other man's touch but his. His heart demanded answers.

"Hey, you. I was hoping you'd drop by." She leaned against the door, her seductive eyes raking over him. Was she playing him?

His whole body came alive under her gaze. Her smell

wound around him, pulling him towards her as he stepped inside.

"Are you okay?" she asked, as if sensing his inner turmoil. "Who was that?"

Mia's brow furrowed before understanding flashed across her beautiful face. "My friend from California flew in for the day."

Was this friend in on the benefits too? "Do you kiss all your friends?"

The side of her mouth quirked up. "Only the very best ones." She headed towards the back of the house and he followed, anger tensing every muscle in his rigid body. Disgust roiled in his belly and jealousy clamored, battering the inside of his rib cage.

His ears rang as she opened the patio doors and walked into the humid night air. The pool glowed, casting her in a blue hue.

He ground his teeth. How could she be so nonchalant about this while he was feeling like a caged animal, roaring and clawing to get out of its prison?

"Mia." His voice rose in volume with his frustration.

"Yeah?" The silk robe she wore swished to the ground, leaving her naked. The moonlight highlighted the dips and curves of her voluptuous body.

His breath caught in his throat as he struggled to swallow. She stepped into the water, her bare breasts hovering just above the surface, tempting him to forget everything and join her.

No. He wouldn't be caught under her spell. He needed to know.

"Did you fuck him?"

Chapter 22

Mia

Jealousy poured off Andre in waves. Was she a bad person because she wanted to make him squirm just a little longer? "Did you fuck him?" he grated like his throat was full of gravel. The look that flashed in his eyes stole any mirth she'd had at his expense. Pain.

"No. But it really wouldn't be any of your business if I did." She moved her finger between them. "We're not dating."

Andre's shoulders lowered as whatever tension he brought with him dissipated. A whoosh of air left his mouth as he scrubbed a hand over his face. An ache formed in her chest. It had been a while since anyone cared about her, and even though this man only wanted her body, it felt good knowing she was wanted by him. *For now, anyways.*

"This is no strings," he agreed. "But we're exclusive."

She smiled and paddled her hands beneath the warm water. "That sounds an awful lot like a relationship."

"I thought you didn't want a relationship?" His dark eyebrows rose questioningly.

"I don't. But you can't have it both ways. Adding exclusivity means more room to develop feelings."

Andre sighed before stripping off his shirt and pants until

he was only in his black boxer briefs. He stepped into the water, sending ripples into the pool. His muscular form in the soft aqua glow highlighted every chiseled plane and ridge of his toned body, down to his thick, strong thighs. Strength and power exuded from the man. Her body ached, the throb getting stronger as he walked towards her in the pool. His hands reached out, taking her face in his large palms. How was it possible to feel fear of vulnerability and comfort at the same time?

"I want to continue what we have. No strings."

The intensity of his gaze mixed with the flutter of emotions battering her insides at his touch. His closeness was dizzying. Heat flashed through her body, singeing her self-control.

"But I also want exclusivity and honesty. Don't hide shit from me. You want to be with another man, then we'll end this and go our separate ways. I won't be fucking you and sharing your body with anyone else. I. Don't. Share. Are we clear?" His deep voice growled his last words.

Andre's touch burned her flesh with want and need. After the events of the day with Mateo, she'd been reminded yet again why everything in her life was temporary. Yes, she could give this to Andre. She'd enjoy it while it lasted and hope he didn't hate her when it was all over.

She nodded.

"Say it," he commanded.

She glanced at his full lips, and licked her own. "I won't fuck anyone but you."

His mouth clamped on her neck as she gasped. His touch became rough and feverish. He tasted like whiskey and determination. This was the first Andre she'd slept with. Raw and needy. Untamed and reckless. Fucking—that was what this was. Pure and simple. Why did her heart ache at the thought? She pushed the question aside, along with all the other uncomfortable feelings that bubbled up in his presence. She locked them away deep down with all her secrets that had never seen the light of day.

His hands roamed over her breasts, pinching her nipples as his suction on her neck increased, blurring the lines between pleasure and pain as need blanketed her.

She moaned.

His mouth released as he looked at her and smirked. "Now everyone will know you're off-limits."

She reached for the semi-sore spot where his mouth had been. "You left a mark?"

"I'm just getting started." His mouth crashed onto hers, his sweet tongue darting in her mouth. She wrapped her arms around him as they became a frantic knot of hands and legs. He picked her up and carried her out of the pool. She never stopped kissing him as they slipped through the back door of her house, the dripping water making the tiles slippery. She gripped him tighter as he turned towards the stairs. Not needing light to find it, he made his way to her bedroom. He laid her on the bed before flicking the bedside lamp on.

"I wanna see you," he said. Like she needed an explanation.

He stripped his wet boxers off before hungrily raking his eyes over her exposed body. "I also want you to see who's gonna fuck you so hard you're gonna feel me for a week. I'm gonna make you come so much you won't ever need to consider another man in your bed."

If she was wearing panties, they would have melted. She could have gotten caught on the fact that he used the word *ever*, as if he expected this thing between them to last much longer than it could. But there was a very gorgeous naked man crawling over her, his hard cock pressing into her soft flesh. She could think later, because right now, she would get lost in this moment. That was all she could afford. Right now. And she wanted him to make good on every single one of those promises.

"You say you're a man of your word." She panted, tracing the rigid muscles of his shoulders with one hand as her other stroked his cock as it jerked in her palm. "Show me."

And he did. For hours, he traced every curve and line of her body with his hungry mouth as if he was memorizing it. He teased her, bringing her to the brink of pleasure again and again until she was breathless, writhing, and begging.

She reached for his cock again, but he grabbed her wrists and bolted them to the bed with one hand.

"You don't get to touch me," he growled. "Your body is all mine right now. You can come when I say you can."

His voice was dominant and possessive, turning her insides to goo.

"That sound good to you?" he asked.

That ache inside her chest grew as he checked for her consent.

"I'm yours." It didn't feel like a lie. What she wouldn't give to really belong to a man like him, and in turn he would belong to her. Sadness crept up, bringing the sting of tears to her eyes, and she swallowed the lump of emotion.

His own expression flickered with something before it was gone in an instant—back behind the elusive wall he had raised as he thrust inside her. She cried out from pleasure. The connection was too much. It broke the dam that welled deep within. Euphoria radiated through every cell in her body, and as he held her down, there was nothing she could do but feel it all. Everything she kept locked inside came bursting out. A warm comforting feeling washed over her like a wave, drowning out her fears.

His movements were like an erotic incantation, coaxing her into a state of complete rapture. Breathless, unable to even make a sound, her ears rang. The handsome face above her focused solely on her as his expression grew even more intense. As he inhaled, so did she. His body, pounding hard in and out of her at an even pace, drew out the pleasure. He exhaled, his breath mingling with hers in the small space between the lovers.

"Mia, baby, come."

She was already there, her body spasming again and again as the orgasm rocked through her body.

"Come. Come. Come," he repeated over and over. And her body obeyed. His thrusts increased as he roared in her neck. The room grew dark as she slipped off the edge of bliss into complete all-encompassing euphoria.

* * *

"Mia!" Andre shouted her name, but it sounded like she was underwater.

"Mia! Wake up!" Calloused hands shook her shoulders as she opened her eyes.

She clasped a hand over her face. It came away wet. Why was she wet? The pool, the hot sex, and then . . . blackness.

"Shit. Are you okay?" he asked, his eyebrows were narrowed with concern.

"What happened?" she asked, sitting up. Her body ached in the best of ways. He'd fulfilled all his promises.

"You passed the fuck out. That's what happened." He ran his hand over her forehead. "You feeling okay now? Let me get you water." He walked to the bathroom, still completely naked as she checked out his fine ass from behind. She'd passed out?

"Maybe you should go to the hospital."

Panic streaked through her. "No!"

He studied her. She'd overreacted.

"I mean, I'm sure I'm fine. I'm awake now." She took the water and gulped down a few sips. "See? All better."

"Has that happened to you before?" he asked, sitting next to her.

"Um . . ." Should she lie? "A few times. It's nothing, really."

"Blacking out isn't nothing." He climbed into the bed next to her, scooping her into his arms. "Was it the sex? Was it because of something I did?"

She smiled, hoping it would set him more at ease. His heart was thudding against her shoulder pressed against his chest.

"You need an ego boost? Yes, Dre. You're so good at sex you made me black out."

He let out a breath and chuckled. "Well, that's a first for me."

"Me too. From sex, I mean." Every other time it had happened it was because she was feeling too much. Her body just shut down.

"You had me worried." He pulled her closer as his lips pressed a kiss to her shoulder.

"Dre?"

"Yeah?"

"Why are you leaking down my leg?"

"Shit."

He'd forgotten a condom, again. She had too though. When they were together like that, logic went out the window.

"I'm so sorry. I got caught up and totally forgot. I swear I wasn't . . . I mean, fuck. I screwed up."

"It's okay. I forgot too. And I was kind of begging for your cock."

His deep laughter rumbled in his chest, vibrating through her body and sending chills across her skin.

"You certainly were. But that's no excuse. I shouldn't have been so careless. That's the second time it's happened with you. I've never gone bare with anyone else before."

She heard what he didn't say. He'd never let his guard down that completely in the past.

"Me either." She'd not once been so reckless. But the panic never came. She was safe in Andre's arms, shielded from the real world as she reveled in the moment just a little longer.

"Do you need anything from me? I can run to the pharmacy?"

"No. My IUD is as effective as they come, Dre."

"Right. I forgot."

A beat of silence passed. His palm brushed up and down her arm soothingly.

I wish I could keep you.

"I like it when you call me Dre."

"You said only your friends could. I am a friend now. I figured it was allowed," she teased.

"You're something, that's for sure."

"Maybe I should just call you D." She giggled and affected a casual tone. "Hey, D, come on over and give me some of that D." Her laughter grew louder.

"You think you're hilarious, don't you?"

"I try." She sighed.

"You can have this D whenever you want, but only if you *never* refer to me as D. Understood?"

"If I do, do I get punished with the D?"

He snorted. "You'd like that too much."

Anything with this man's cock was a gift. She'd never been one to go crazy over a penis before, but Andre's stretched her so perfectly.

He cleared his throat. "This weekend, my friends are getting together at Remy's house. You wanna come?"

That sounded an awful lot like a date. She shouldn't go, just for that reason. But she wanted to. What did that mean?

"You don't have to. Remy asked if I'd bring you along."

She let out a breath she hadn't realized she was holding. Remy was her friend; so was Jasmine. She'd go to see her friends. *Friends.* Yes, maybe if she thought the word ten more times it would cement into her brain. She'd never had this problem before with guys. There was always a clear line in the sand. Feelings were never mixed with sex. If they were, it was usually from them, and she'd take her cue and run the other way.

"Mia?"

"Sorry, yes. That sounds like fun."

"Let's get cleaned up. I was going to make you dinner before all this happened."

"You were planning to cook for me?" She turned towards him, her belly grumbling at the mention of food.

He grinned sheepishly and shrugged. "I figured it would be nice. You cooked for me, and I wanted to return the favor."

"I'm starving, so how about we have a quick shower?" she agreed.

"Then you better go in there alone, or it might be another hour until we get dinner. Unless—do you need me in there? You know, in case you fall?" he quickly amended.

That ache in her chest was like a sinkhole, getting deeper by the second. He was worried about *her*.

"I'll be fine." She stood and disappeared into the bathroom before he could see the emotion welling up as tears slipped past her defenses and down her cheeks.

* * *

After a quick shower, she went to the bedroom to dress. When she entered, the fresh set of sheets and comforter caught her attention. He'd stripped her bed and then made it for her. A note sat in the center.

Went home to shower and start dinner. Come on over when you're ready. -Dre

"Friends do dinners," she said aloud, trying to convince herself.

Besides, she'd just worked up one hell of an appetite. A tiny voice inside her told her he was the only man to appease it.

Another voice told her to run.

Chapter 23

Mia

"Did you bring the wine?" Andre asked with his back turned to her at the stove.

Mia shut the door behind her. He'd changed into a pair of low-hung sweatpants and a Seaview Construction T-shirt.

"Don't I always?" Mia held up the bottle.

Andre turned and smiled. "Perfect." He picked up a wooden spoon and stirred whatever deliciousness was in the pot making the whole house smell divine—garlic and onion with the rich aroma of a tomato-based sauce.

Mia set the wine on the counter and walked over to peek at the stove. The large pot bubbled with the thick red sauce, and bits of green herbs floated along the surface. "Need any help?"

"How about a taste test?" Andre pulled the spoon from the red sauce and blew on it. Her attention darted to his muscular forearms and the veins running through the sinewy tendons. He shifted his hand as he offered her a sample. Her gaze met his as she bent forward and opened her mouth. Andre's eyes darkened as he brought the sauce to her lips. She moaned at the perfect blend of herbs and tomatoes before licking her lips.

Andre's gaze darted to her mouth just a moment before he tenderly kissed her. The richness of the sauce mixed with his natural sweetness, overloading her senses. This kiss was different than all the ones that had come before. This one was tender. She'd already been sexually satiated, but a new longing built deep within her.

She broke the kiss, staring back into his glazed eyes. *What was that?* "I think it's done."

Andre nodded and shut the stove off. "Pasta is too. Wine opener is in here." He pointed to a row of three drawers before motioning to a cupboard. "And glasses are in there."

Mia pulled open the drawer and found the corkscrew. She was just thankful to have something to keep her hands busy. This all seemed a little too domestic. *But he's been to my house for dinner half a dozen times or more.* So why did this time feel so different?

She poured herself a full glass and took a few big sips before filling his cup. He carried over their plates of steaming spaghetti and meatballs before setting them on the rectangular table off the kitchen. Mia took another sip before joining him. *This is not a date. Just two friends sharing a meal after fucking each other's brains out.*

"I'm so hungry." Mia sat across from him. No need to be too close.

"Well, we did have quite the workout." Andre chuckled.

She laughed before taking another sip of her drink. The alcohol smoothed out the edges and enabled her to relax. She could do this. Friendly banter like they always had on their runs. No need to imagine this was something it wasn't.

They tucked into the food. Andre's gaze never seemed to leave her for too long. She sliced a meatball and stuffed a piece of it in her mouth. "This is really good. How did you learn to cook like this?"

Andre smiled before taking a sip of his own wine. "My parents always took turns doing the cooking. When we were old enough, they'd drag us into the kitchen with them. We had a rule that the cook didn't have to clean. I hate doing dishes, like, loathe that chore." He shrugged. "So, I opted to cook dinner more often than not."

He cleaned up and did my dishes the night of Mamá's birthday though. Somehow knowing it was his least favorite thing made it all that much more meaningful.

"It paid off. This is delicious."

He flashed her a wink. "The secret is love."

She coughed, panic squeezing her chest tight. Andre sat straighter, brows knit together. "Are you okay?"

She nodded, reaching for her wineglass to dislodge the stuck food. Gulping down the alcohol helped in more ways than one.

"Went down the wrong hole," she rasped, patting her chest. The sudden urge to flee rose within her.

He smirked. "I've been around Bently too much for me not to have a comeback for that."

She shook her head. "Boys and your sexual innuendo."

He leaned forward, resting his elbows on the table. "Says the woman who told me that she was going to be the best thing I ever tasted."

She laughed, the tension leaving her chest. "I guess I did, didn't I?"

"You weren't wrong."

She couldn't help but smile. *But I was wrong about the depth of how I could feel for you.* This man had her knocked off her axis.

By the time they'd finished their dinner, she was warm and

relaxed from all the wine, and the laughter. Andre stood and gathered their plates.

"I can do the dishes," Mia offered.

He shook his head. "You're my guest."

"But you helped me last time. And you cooked. It's only fair." She drained the last of her glass and got up to help.

"I guess you could help me." He caved.

They worked side by side. Mia washed and rinsed while Andre dried and put away.

"Let's leave the glasses out. I have another bottle right here." Andre pulled one from the fridge.

She hesitated. Should she stay?

He popped the cork and poured two generous helpings before passing her a glass. She glanced out his window towards her dark empty house. What could one more glass hurt?

Mia followed him into the living room and took a seat on his comfy couch, tucking her feet under her before she sipped again from her glass. He settled next to her, his hand gripping her knee. Even though she'd just had the man an hour ago, fire burned up her leg from his touch, igniting a blaze of something between lust and comfort. The alcohol hit her, adding a floaty, relaxed feeling to the mix.

"You're a pretty cool person," Andre said.

"You're not so bad yourself."

"Truth or dare?" he asked.

She shook her head. "What are we, in middle school?"

He laughed. "Come on. It will be fun."

She rolled her eyes. "Dare."

His eyes glimmered in the low light of the living room. "I dare you to tell me one of your fantasies."

"Going right for the deep questions, huh?" She laughed,

tipping her head to the side. The room tilted as she set down her near-empty glass of wine. Threading her fingers into his, she licked her lips and met his gaze. Flashes of children running around as she and the imagined Prince Charming snuggled up together played through her mind. *Prince Charming could look an awful lot like Andre.* She shook her head, trying to rid herself of the impossible.

"I've always wanted to try semi-public sex. You know, like, where someone would just have to look up and see you or walk through the door. I imagine it would add a little extra something."

He took a drink and nodded.

"What about you? Truth or dare?" She relaxed against the back of the sofa, spreading her legs over his lap.

Andre's big hands grasped her feet, massaging them. "Truth."

"Mmmm." She tried to focus, but the things that man could do with his hands . . .

"Mia?"

"Why were you so mean to me?" What exactly had caused this man to hate her so much without even getting to know her?

His hands halted as he sighed. Andre's eyes met hers. "Because you scared me. I felt that spark between us, and you are so goddamn sexy. You made me want you when I'd sworn off women. You made it impossible for my life to continue the way it was in my comfort level. I got angry at myself and took it out on you. Sorry again about being an asshole."

She nodded. "I get that." Boy, did she ever.

"Your turn." He pressed his thumb into the arch of her foot and resumed the massage.

God, she could lie here like this forever.

Whoa. Don't get too comfortable. This is just temporary.

"Truth."

"What do you want out of life?"

Wasn't that a loaded question. "I just want security. And to find happiness. To honor my parents' memory."

He nodded, not taking his eyes off her. It was like he knew she was just scratching the surface, that she was holding back. "I pick dare."

This game was becoming all too real. "I dare you to kiss me." *Help me feel not so alone for a little while.*

Andre grabbed her hand, pulling her onto his lap as she straddled him. His hands gently but firmly grasped her face. Her eyes fluttered closed. Anticipation wound thick between them as his breath tickled against her lips. She closed the distance, melding her mouth to his. Soft lips, hot tongues, and chemistry sparked like fireworks on the Fourth of July, lighting her up inside. Tears escaped the corner of her eyes. What was this man doing to her? Maybe it was the wine. Maybe she was drunk on Andre. Either way, this was too much and not enough all at once.

One of his palms moved to the back of her neck, gripping and holding her closer while the other traced her spine.

The way he held her was like he cherished her. Like he cared for her. She gripped his shirt, pulling him closer and holding him at a distance all at the same time. Breaking the kiss was harder than it should have been. "I should go."

"Stay?" he asked, chest heaving against hers.

She glanced at the stairs, hesitating.

"I promise I'll make it worth your while." He nipped at her shoulder, as heady tingles shot through her.

What could it hurt? As long as they had sex, it wouldn't

mean anything more, right? His touch blurred lines. What-ever this feeling was between them was more like controlled disorder. She was on the verge of combustion even though she'd just had him hours ago. Yet still, Mia wanted him. She couldn't walk away from this.

"Okay." Her voice was just above a whisper.

Andre dug his hands into her hips and stood, lifting her in his arms as she wrapped her legs around his waist and giggled.

The man was chaos and she couldn't get enough. She'd hang on just a little longer, stealing what happiness she could and locking it away for the dark days to come. Because they would come. They always did.

Chapter 24

Mia

The cookout was in full swing. The scent of roasting meat and smoke from the grill wafted over Remy's backyard. Three picnic tables had been moved together to form one long table filled with several delectable dishes.

"You've really outdone yourself, Remy. I don't know where you find the time or energy to do all this," Mia complimented.

Remy smiled and adjusted her baby boy on her hip. His little light brown fist grabbed one of her long braids. "I love doing this. Mikel helped me prep most of it last night after we got the kids in bed. Emma and I finished it up this morning. Have you met her yet?"

Mia shook her head.

Remy waved her hand for Mia to follow. "Come on over here. I'll introduce you."

Mia glanced towards the grill where Andre stared at her, sipping on a beer with both Mikel and Bently at his sides. He offered her a secret smile as her belly flip-flopped. Darting her eyes back ahead, Remy stood by two pretty blond women she hadn't seen around before.

"Mia, this is Emma. We've been best friends forever." Remy

smiled at the woman closest to her. Emma stretched out one tattooed arm which Mia gladly shook. "Nice to meet you."

"I've heard a lot about you. Rem doesn't shut up about your cookies. This is my girlfriend, Roxy."

The other woman waved before wrapping her arm around Emma's waist protectively.

"Hello. It's great to meet new people." Mia smiled.

"Mia is going to run a new yoga studio in town," Remy said to Emma.

Roxy's blue eyes looked her up and down as if sizing her up. "Yoga, huh?"

"Yeah."

"That's really cool. Maybe we can check it out together once it opens," Emma suggested, placing her arm around her girlfriend as well. Roxy seemed to relax a little.

Mia's skin tingled. She turned in time to catch Andre's stare once again. He winked before angling back to Mikel and saying something. They both laughed.

"Earth to Mia," Remy said. Mia snapped her attention back to her friend. Emma and Roxy were now walking towards the coolers of beer. How long had she been ogling Andre? Remy's grin told her it was long enough to be caught.

"Are we going to talk about the elephant in the room?" Remy asked as Lyra darted around them and then ran back to her swing set.

"What do you mean?"

Remy rolled her eyes. "I think he really likes you too. Just be patient with him. He's had his fair share of heartbreak."

The concern that flashed in her friend's eyes brought an ache to Mia's chest. The thought of Andre, a man she'd once seen as her enemy, now her . . . *friend*, brought a surge of protective need in her. "We're just friends."

"Oh, so you have nothing to do with the smile that's been plastered on his face lately? My usually grumpy, ornery brother is just magically happy?" Remy gave her an incredulous look.

"Why would you assume it's because of me?" Mia shrugged, trying to act nonchalant. Knowing she might have something to do with the happiness returning to Andre's life made her chest squeeze with pride.

"Oh, nothing besides neither one of you can keep your eyes off each other." Remy giggled. "I know my brother, and I know that look in his eye. He *really* likes you." The last sentence sounded a bit like a warning.

"We are just friends. Trust me when I say that's all we can ever be. He's not interested in me like that. He's made that very clear."

"And you?" Remy asked.

What about Mia? Did she want more with Andre? It didn't matter, so there was no use entertaining the idea because it could *never* happen.

"Come get your grub!" Bently bellowed.

Mia hooked her hand around Remy's free arm as baby Phoenix snuggled against her shoulder with drooping eyes. "Come on. Let's go eat."

"Okay, but this conversation isn't over." Remy laughed.

Mia sat as the group passed around each bowl of various salads, sides, and platters of grilled meat. She helped herself to a little of everything. A cold beer appeared in front of her, Andre's muscular dark arm lingering just a beat longer as his other hand moved to her waist. Mia flushed from the contact, her body sparking alive. She searched the table, fearing all eyes would be on her. Only Remy gave a knowing smile, nodding her acknowledgement before she adjusted her shirt to nurse the baby.

"You looked parched." Andre's deep voice vibrated through her body, stirring up another kind of thirst.

"Thank you." She fought the urge to turn and kiss him.

His friends bantered back and forth, but she tuned them out as he sat beside her, his hand resting on her thigh. She'd woken in his bed this morning sore in all the right places. Wrapped against his warm chest with sunlight peeking through the blinds was how she'd want to wake up every day if she had the choice. *But I don't.*

"I still can't believe you did that," Andre said.

Mia glanced around the table, coming back to the conversation. "Did what?"

Bently leaned his elbows on the table as he smirked. "Your boy, Dre, here had just broken up with his high-school sweetheart. He was moping around, barely eating. So, as the good friend that I am, I set him up with a prom date."

The laughter that burst out of Mikel signaled there was much more to this story than he was letting on.

"That's putting it lightly." Andre shook his head.

Bently shrugged. "Ruby Wentworth. She had the biggest crush on Dre."

"She had pictures from my yearbook plastered all over her locker and taped together with her face to make it look like we were a couple," Andre added dryly.

"I set up the most romantic scene in the cafeteria. Rose petals—the whole shebang. Every girl that wandered in hoped this display was for them," Bently continued, his face shining with pride. "I even got the kitchen staff in on it."

"So, what happened?" Mia asked, before taking another bite of her food.

"I had Mikel distract Dre outside until I gave the signal," Bently answered.

Mikel wiped a tear from his eye as he kept laughing. "You should have seen your face when you realized what was happening. Wish we had camera phones back then."

Dre just shook his head.

"I professed the most beautiful sonnet. Made a big show of all the mushy cheesy lines I could think of. At the very end, just as Mikel ushered Andre inside—thrusting a bouquet of roses in his hand—I announced that Andre wanted Ruby to be his date to prom." Bently beamed.

"Did you embarrass the poor girl?" Was she a casualty in their prank?

"Nah, she was beaming," Mikel answered.

"What happened after that?" Mia looked at Andre.

"I took Ruby to prom," Dre said dryly. Her respect for the man grew.

"My man would never let a woman down. Ruby was good people." Bently shoveled a big bite of macaroni salad into his mouth.

"Then why didn't you take her to prom?" Mikel asked.

Bently rolled his eyes. "Because I'd already promised Stacy, Victoria, and Jenna that I'd take them."

"You had three prom dates?" Mia asked, bewildered.

"The more the merrier." Bently grinned.

Mia shook her head.

"Yeah, he probably came home with three dates too— herpes, chlamydia, and HPV," Emma added.

Everyone laughed as Bently scowled.

"What's her-piss, Mama?" Lyra asked.

Remy shot Emma a look of disapproval. "It's a disease, honey."

Lyra's face grew worried. "Is Uncle Bently gonna get sick again?"

Bently got up from the table and walked around to Lyra, taking her in his arms. "No, baby. Aunty Emma was making a joke. I'm not sick anymore. I'm all better, remember?"

Anymore?

"That's not a funny joke," Lyra said.

"I agree. How about this one? How do you get a tissue to dance?" Bently asked holding the growing girl in his arms.

"How?" she asked.

"You put a little boogie in it."

Lyra giggled. "Your jokes are funny, Uncle Bently."

"I know. Not everyone can be as awesome as me." He set her back down between her parents before he stuck his tongue out at Emma, who slipped him the middle finger discreetly.

The table began their chatter as if nothing had happened. Everyone laughed and joked, seeming to be more aware of the little ears listening.

After lunch, Lyra convinced Mia to join the game of freeze tag. Mia squealed as Remy chased her, darting behind a tree. Two big arms grabbed her, pinning her to Andre's chest.

"Let me go before she gets here!" Mia yelped.

"No way. I'm using you as my human shield," Andre said, not loosening his grasp as she struggled.

"Cheater!"

He growled in her ear, "I believe you started the cheating that first day we raced. I told you I'd get you back."

Remy ran around the tree, her arms outstretched. The

moment Remy's hand touched her was the same instant Andre let go.

"I got you both!" Remy yelled, pumping her fist in the air before running off.

Andre gave an exaggerated pout.

Mia smirked, out of breath. "That's what you get for trying to break the rules."

Andre wrapped his arms around her waist, pulling her against his body. He dragged her behind a large maple tree, his arousal poking her backside. "Maybe this is exactly what I wanted. It's been fucking torture seeing you floating around this backyard wearing these tiny red shorts." His hand squeezed her ass. "And don't even get me started on this white tank top. All I want to do is—" He dipped his head and licked along her neck to between her breasts. She pressed against his chest as her own arousal seeped onto her panties.

"Stop. Someone is going to see us." She turned her head to search the area for any witnesses—just foliage and green grass.

"Isn't that what you wanted?" His voice deepened.

My fantasy. She squeezed her thighs together, sure that her panties were wet. "You're insatiable."

"If you hadn't left my house in such a hurry this morning, maybe I'd be a little less needy now." He traced her lips with his thumb.

"I see. So, it's my fault?"

He shrugged. "Hey, you said it. Not me."

She chuckled before leaning in and brushing her lips softly over his.

"Game over! I got everyone," Remy announced, breaking their moment.

Mia backed away from Andre, the lust in his eyes only

adding fuel to the fire now raging inside her. She ran away from him, from the feelings that had awoken in his presence. His heavy footfalls were just behind her as they returned to the rest of the group. Mikel handed them each a water bottle before Andre slumped to the ground.

Mia continued until she was across from him in the circle of friends. She needed to put some distance between them. His eyes continued to focus on only her as if she was all he saw. The more time she spent with him, the more she could see herself falling for someone like Dre.

He really likes you. Remy's words repeated in her mind. Even if he wanted more, once he found out she'd lied by omission, it would be over. He'd made it clear he hated liars. She'd be better off making the most of the time they had now. She closed her eyes as the sunshine warmed her skin. Mia would enjoy it while it lasted until the clouds came.

A tumble of mixed emotions clamored around inside her. Happiness and fear. Contentment and anxiety. Guilt weighed heavily on her shoulders as she opened her eyes and surveyed the group.

Bently sat next to her. "I'll accept your gratitude in the form of a party where you are the cook."

She turned to him. "What?"

He nodded towards Andre. "Your boy just needed a little push in the right direction. Sometimes a man needs some competition to spur him into action. Like this." He draped his arm around her.

A throat clearing made her glance up. Andre stood in front of her, reaching out his hand. "Let's go get a cold beer, Mia."

Mia glanced back to Bently who had the same smirk that was damn near permanently plastered on his face.

"I expect authentic Mexican cuisine." Bently dropped his arm as she grasped Andre's hand.

She got to her feet, the need radiating off Andre singeing her skin. Andre didn't let go of her hand as he led her into the house. This was too much. Bently and Remy were right. Andre was getting too attached. *She* was getting too attached. Her heart and mind were screaming two very different things. *This is all just sex.* And she'd prove it.

She pulled Andre into the bathroom and closed the door, flicking the lock.

"Wha—"

Mia cut off his question as she popped his pants button and tugged the zipper down. She needed him to fuck her—hard. Remind her what this was all about. No feelings other than lust. No time to think, just experience. She shoved the ball of emotion welling up inside her down as she freed his cock from his boxers.

"Condom. Now." She pulled off her shorts and panties as he sheathed himself in latex.

His hands dipped into her sex, the contact making her knees wobble as she tried to regain control. She pushed his hand away.

"No. I just need you to fuck me." She spun so that her back was turned to him as she gripped the marble sink.

He nudged between her folds and slid inside slowly. Too gentle.

"Fuck me hard and fast," she whimpered in frustration, fighting the war inside her chest. He pounded into her as she struggled to breathe. She bent, allowing him deeper access. Mia needed the pain today. She wanted the raw animalistic mating, not anything close to making love.

"Like this? Is this how you imagined it in your fantasy?" he asked.

"Harder."

"I'm gonna come if I keep going," he warned.

"Then come." This was just sex.

"Ladies first." He was flirting with her. Trying to give her everything he thought she wanted. No, this was just sex. He was using her and she was using him. She needed a good reminder of that.

"I will. Just don't stop," she lied.

He thrust, faster and harder as Mia bit back the tears. She forced herself to ignore the building pleasure and focus on the carnage of her past. The blood on her hands. He could never know. No one could. And because of that, she'd punish herself until she remembered her place.

"I'm coming." His body tensed.

"Yes," she commanded.

Andre pulled out, kissing her shoulder.

She shook her head. "Why did you stop?"

"Because you haven't come yet." His hand reached to cup her breast and pinch her nipple as his other found her clit.

"No. I just want you to fuck me."

"Baby, it's no fun if you don't come. That's my favorite part."

Baby. The endearment snapped something inside her. Her orgasm was his favorite part? Not his own? What had she gotten herself into?

She struggled to suck in a breath. The room grew dim. *No.* She couldn't do this here. Her heartbeat raced in her chest as she grabbed her clothes and redressed hurriedly.

She needed to get out of there. She needed air. She needed to run.

"Mia—"

"I need to go. Tell Remy something came up." Mia pulled the bathroom door open and darted out, not willing to wait another second. She had to escape before the panic attack hit her in full force. She never should have started anything with Andre. This had to end now.

Chapter 25

Andre

Walking across the grass of her front lawn in the fading light, Andre's stomach knotted. Concern for Mia squeezed his chest as he knocked on the door.

Would she answer? What had he done to upset her?

Slow steps padded closer as her silhouette formed on the other side of the glass. He drew in a steadying breath as she opened the door. Her face was impassive, her eyes void of emotion.

"Did you need something?" she asked, her voice unwavering and indifferent.

"Are you okay?" he asked. Was she going to invite him in?

"Of course."

He nodded towards her house. "Can we talk for a minute?"

She bit her bottom lip and looked down. "I'm really tired. I just want to be alone tonight. I'm not in the mood for sex."

He blinked a few times, digesting what was happening. She was pushing him away, reminding him where the lines were drawn. Or did she feel used because this was just sex? Did she really want more?

"I never got to tell you about my visit with Aaron at the Hope Facility." Hopefully a neutral topic would set her at ease.

She hesitated, searching his eyes before standing aside and gesturing him in. Mia closed the door behind him and crossed her arms over herself.

Should he reach out and embrace her? Should he ignore the elephant in the room or directly address it?

"Coffee?" she asked.

"Nah, too late in the day for me."

She nodded and walked over to her gray overstuffed couch.

He sat next to her, giving her a little space between them. "Aaron said he'd keep an eye out for the kid, and ask around. But he didn't know anyone off the top of his head that fit the description and had a sister."

Mia nodded as she stared at the coffee table, seemingly avoiding his eyes.

"He also said there is a rise in gang activity in the area. You gotta be safe, Mia—no chancing walking alone at night or in certain areas of town. Tell me what time you start running and I'll go with you, just in case."

Her fists clenched as she angled her body farther away from him. How did this happen? They'd had a great day. She'd fit in with his friends better than any other person. His ex hadn't even tried. Mia was playful, kind, genuine, and thoughtful. *Shit*. He wanted more. He wanted a relationship with Mia. Could he open himself up like that and take a chance on her?

"I don't need you to. I can take care of myself," Mia said.

He was already in too deep, because the thought of not protecting her made the depths of his soul ache. His chest burned, anger rising from its hidden recesses. Fuck. If he exploded, he'd push her away. What did she need? "Okay. But promise me you'll be careful."

She turned to look at him. "I always am." The mask she

wore slipped only a moment before she steeled her gaze and focused on her hands in her lap.

Maybe he needed to man up and take the first step. "I dated my ex, Tiffany, for five years. I came home one day and she was crying in the kitchen, which was no rare event. She always demanded my attention, and at the slightest thing I did or didn't do, she'd turn it into this big production of waterworks and packing her stuff."

Mia relaxed into the couch, lifting her eyes to his chest.

"I really thought I loved her. I figured all relationships had their fair share of ups and downs. I guess we just had more lows. Anyways, that last day she told me she was pregnant."

Mia's eyes darted to him, the question radiating from them.

"I was shocked and terrified, but also excited. We hadn't planned on having a kid anytime soon. We'd always used protection. So, I figured it was meant to be."

She winced.

He took a calming breath and steadied himself, the wounds still fresh from that day. "She told me it wasn't mine. She'd been cheating on me for the better part of a year."

Mia reached out her hand, placing it on his knee. Her touch was a balm, offering him comfort. He placed his palm over hers, rubbing the soft flesh with his thumb. Could she feel this too? The fact that they just seemed to fit?

"I'm sorry."

"I'm glad it happened. I would have made a very bad choice to remain in a relationship that wasn't healthy if she hadn't told me. I would have married her and stayed forever." It was the first time he could fully admit it and see the positive about the situation.

"Do you still have feelings for her?" Mia asked.

He sighed and rubbed the back of his neck with his free hand. "Maybe a small part of me continues to grieve the relationship that we could have had. I don't wish her any ill will. But it's too late for us. I'm not the same man I was. She's not the woman I want." He locked eyes with her. Would she understand his meaning? Mia was the only woman he wanted now. He trusted her.

Mia nodded. "Thank you for sharing with me."

"I'm here to listen to you too." He cupped her face softly in his hands.

Her gaze wavered as she took a deep breath. "Good to know."

"You want to tell me what happened earlier?"

Mia pulled away. "It's just sex."

Was she reminding him or herself? If he told her it was beginning to be more to him, would she run the other way?

"You were upset."

Her dark eyes burned with anger as she stood. "I wanted you to fuck me and you stopped."

He remained seated, trying to stay calm. Fighting the urge to defend himself at her absurd anger, he counted to ten in his head. She was looking for a fight. She wanted to push him away. Anytime he lost his temper around her, he ended up hurting her and that was the last thing he wanted to do. "You'd be the only woman alive who got angry at a man who finished without making her come at least once."

She crossed her arms, her breathing becoming shallow. Her jaw clenched as if she didn't know how to respond.

Tell me the truth.

"I'm not an asshole who uses women up. Especially people I care about, like my friends."

Her shoulders dropped and her jaw relaxed. His word choice seemed to put her at ease.

She sighed and sat next to him again. "I know."

He draped his arm around her and pulled her into his chest. She just felt right. Like another piece of himself that had been missing for all his life. All his assumptions about her had been wrong. He'd been too scared to admit it before, but the reason he'd hated her was because he could end up falling in love with her. Not that he was there yet. Hell, did he even know what love was? He'd thought he'd loved Tiffany, and look where that had gotten him.

He kissed her forehead and breathed in her coffee-colored hair. Her sweet and spicy scent was intoxicating. His body reacted to her very presence. He wanted to worship her and give her all the pleasure she could handle. He'd show Mia the reverence she deserved.

"Why don't you come over? I'll reheat the pasta from last night and then we can finish what we started or do nothing at all—if that's what you want," he suggested.

Mia pulled away. "Not tonight. I'm really tired."

He searched her face, tucking a loose tendril of hair behind her ear. He leaned in and kissed her cheeks before leaving a peck on her nose. She smiled, and the beautiful sight sent a bolt of energy straight through his body. Whatever magic between them was conjured up by this woman alone, and no part of him wanted to leave through that front door unless she was coming with him. "Want me to run you a bath?"

Her brows formed a triangle as if she was surprised.

"I can run a mean bubble bath." He grinned, hoping he'd set her at ease.

She hesitated, before answering, "I can do it. I appreciate the offer though."

"Anytime." He kissed her, slowly, tenderly. Mia melted into his arms as he sucked her bottom lip into his mouth, caressing her tongue with his own before releasing her. Her eyes shone with unshed tears as she blinked rapidly, fighting them off.

"You sure you don't need me to stay?" *Let me in.*

Mia nodded. "I'm just going to take that bath you suggested and call it an early night."

"Okay. If that's what you need." He turned and walked away despite the tether between them tugging him back towards her. Mia had been patient and supportive of his boundaries. Now it was time he did the same. Because one thing was for certain. He wanted more with Mia, and he'd wait until she was ready.

Chapter 26

Mia

After stirring the red chili sauce, Mia added a pinch more salt. The savory aroma of slow-cooked pork with the array of spices blanketed her in comfort. If she closed her eyes, she could pretend it was her mother cooking beside her.

"I miss you, Mamá."

Mia shut the stove off and stepped away, walking over to the back porch. Opening the double doors, she took deep breaths as she tried to ground herself in the present. The crisp September air in New Hampshire was clean and earthy. She surveyed the backyard, all set up for her new friends with picnic tables. The sunshine reflected off the turquoise water of her pool, where no doubt Remy's daughter would want to go for a swim. It should warm up by the time they all arrived later that afternoon.

It had been weeks since the incident in the bathroom. Mia avoided the work site unless absolutely needed. She'd had to begin the detachment—it was best for both of them. Andre was respectful of that. *Because it is only sex to him. I'm the one who's catching feelings.*

Mia sat with her head in her hands. Birds chirped in the trees lining the back of her house. She looked up towards his house. Movement in his bedroom window caught her eye. His half-naked body appeared and then moved out of sight a moment later. Lust stirred to life—just as it did every time she laid eyes on the man. He didn't even have to be there to have her hot and bothered, because thinking about him made her just as flammable. She'd resist giving in to her body's demands as she had for the most part of the last few weeks. Mia had only let Andre into her bed a handful of times. It would be easier if he texted.

The soft padding of feet across the grass made her look over her shoulder.

Andre set a paper bag and a coffee cup next to her on the porch with a warm smile. "Wanted to bring you some breakfast before I headed out for a run."

She eyed his bare chest, down to the V disappearing into his running shorts. Swallowing hard, she managed a, "Thank you."

"See you later." He winked and then kissed her forehead before he was off. She admired his tight ass until he was out of sight.

Why did he have to be so perfect?

If she had been born in this country, she'd pursue him in a heartbeat. Her mother would have loved him. *Oh, Mamá. How am I to navigate these treacherous seas without you?* Life was like walking across a floor of broken glass—dangerous and brutal. One wrong turn could shred her to pieces.

Chimes rang from her pocket. She pulled out the phone. *Mateo.*

"*Hola, hermoso.*"

"Hello to you too, beautiful," his deep voice said.

"How are you?"

"I'm missing my favorite girl."

She smiled as her spirit lightened. "I miss you too. When are you going to come visit me again?"

"That's actually why I'm calling. I have some time coming up soon. I can finally take a break at work and come see you next week. Does that work?"

"That's perfect! Are you bringing your sister?" Mia asked.

"Do I have to share you? I was hoping it would be just the two of us again."

"Of course you have to bring her. I haven't seen her since I moved." Mia laughed.

"Well, if you hadn't relocated to the other side of the country, we could see a lot more of each other. I miss your beautiful face every day. After all, we have quite the event to finish planning in the coming months."

Right. How could she forget?

Because she wanted to live in her fantasy land a little longer with Andre in her bed.

"You know why I had to leave," she reminded him.

He sighed. "I know, honey. I just wished you'd let me take care of you—more than what I'm doing now."

Mia fought the tears as she shook her head. "I have to do this myself. You're giving me exactly what I need right now. I'm already asking so much of you."

"Anything for you. You're so important to me. And soon . . ."

Mia smiled. "And soon, so much more."

"Alright. I've got to get back to work. Love you."

"Love you too."

Mia ended the call. A pressure built—an uneasy feeling chilling her insides. A warning blared in the back of her mind.

There was a fork in the road ahead that she'd never seen coming. How did she choose? She couldn't. That choice had been taken from her the moment she was born south of the border.

Ding-dong!

Mia stood and made her way to the front door. Drawing a deep breath, she opened it.

Her eyes lazily made the ascent from his black Chucks to the fitted jeans that clung to his muscular thighs. A black T-shirt showed off his toned arms from his physically demanding job. The need to fall into them was overwhelming. He'd offer her reprieve from her life—her real life—not the fantasy she lived while with him.

"Hey. Just thought you could use some help prepping for the party later."

Andre's deep voice sent heat pooling between her thighs. It had been six long days since she'd last given in to temptation. Unbidden thoughts tumbled into her mind, pulling her left and right. His presence intoxicated her like no other. The magnetic tug towards him was stronger than the force of gravity. She yearned for him, every cell in her body craving his touch.

"I could use something from you." She ran her finger over his mouth and down his chest slowly as she locked her gaze with his. Lust burned her from the tiny contact.

Andre leaned in and kissed her, chasing away all the warring thoughts from her mind and bringing her back to the present where only his body against hers mattered. The door slammed shut as he walked her backwards. She gasped. Andre picked Mia up in his arms and carried her up the stairs. They entered the room where he set her down carefully on the bed. She broke the kiss to close her bedroom door, shutting out reality for a little longer.

* * *

Two hours later, they were both downstairs. She laughed as he spread the filling in the tamale and passed it to her. He'd given up trying to wrap them himself.

He sipped his beer. "See? We make a great team."

"We do." She smiled, still high on oxytocin and endorphins from the amazing sex. How was it possible that each time got better and better? They did work well together—in and out of the bedroom. Of all the people she'd first met in Shattered Cove, she'd never have guessed that this man would be the one she fit with the most.

"What time will everyone be here?"

Ding-dong!

They both laughed. "I guess that's your answer." She dried her hands on a towel before heading over to the door.

Remy greeted her first, with Lyra next to her and Mikel holding Phoenix behind them. "Hey, girl! We brought some dishes to share."

"Perfect. Come on in. I figured we'd set up the food in the kitchen and eat in the backyard." Mia ushered them in as Andre approached from behind and wrapped an arm around her waist.

"Mommy said you have a pool?" Lyra asked wide-eyed with a floaty in her hand.

Mia nodded. "I sure do."

"After we eat, okay, pumpkin?" Mikel reminded her.

"Oooookayyyy." She walked in, guided by her father.

"Is the food in the car?" Andre asked Remy, slipping his

hand into the back pocket of Mia's skinny jeans. Heat flared up her body. Did he even realize what he was doing to her?

"Yes. There are a few dishes in the trunk."

Andre disappeared out the door, leaving Mia alone in the entryway with a smirking Remy.

"Make yourself at home," Mia said.

"Mm-hmm. I'm gonna pretend you don't look like you just had sexy time with my brother."

"How did you know?" Mia pressed her neck. Had Andre left a mark on her again?

Remy's smile widened. "I didn't until you just confirmed it."

Mia shook her head. "I walked right into that one."

"See? I knew you two were good for each other." Remy beamed before she hugged her.

"We're just friends."

"Sure." Remy nodded, but her expression was anything but belief.

"Smells delicious in here," Mikel said as he opened the back door. "I'm gonna take these rug rats outside to run around."

"Of course. I put out some toys and art stuff to help keep them occupied," Mia called after him.

Andre came in with an armful of stacked casserole dishes. "Where do you want them?"

Mia directed him to an empty counter as Jasmine, baby Zoey, and Bently entered.

"The party has arrived!" Bently announced, carrying a case of beer.

"Hey, guys," Jasmine said, reaching out her free hand to hug Mia.

"Hello. How's Miss Zoey today?" Mia asked.

"She's great."

Two strong arms wrapped around Mia and picked her up in a bear hug. "Hey, beautiful. You've really pulled out all the stops for me. Smells so good in here. Almost as good as you," Bently said.

"Let her go, asshole," Andre said.

Bently didn't move. "Nah, I think I like her like this. She's so light, I could carry her around for hours."

Mia smacked his chest. "Okay, playboy. Put me down or the food's gonna burn."

"Ouch! Hit me where it hurts why don't you," Bently teased.

Mia chuckled and shook her head as she made her way back to the kitchen.

Andre growled from behind. She turned around, startled by the guttural noise. Andre glared at Bently who had the biggest shit-eating grin on his face.

Mia angled back to Remy. "What did I miss?"

"Just my brother staking his claim." Remy laughed.

Jasmine gave Zoey to Bently. "Any more testosterone in here and I'm gonna suffocate. Take this princess outside to play with her cousins."

"Okay. I can see when I'm not wanted." Bently headed towards the backyard.

"You too," Remy said to Andre.

Andre shot Mia a parting look before he followed after his friend.

"Finally! Now we can have some girl time without these macho men interrupting." Remy sighed.

Mia smiled. "Margaritas, anyone?"

"I'll take two." Jasmine laughed.

Mia showed them how to finish prepping the tamales before she got to work making the drinks. Having her kitchen full of her friends brought a fullness to her chest. These women had become like best friends.

After pulling out her own finished array of Mexican meals, Mia slipped Remy's dishes into the oven to warm them up. Sipping the cool, sweet and tangy drinks, Mia relaxed into easy conversation with the women. She left once to let Emma in.

"Sorry I'm late."

"No worries. We're just chatting while we finish prepping the meal." Mia gestured to an empty stool.

"Where's your girlfriend? She let you off your leash to come to this party alone?" Remy asked.

Emma rolled her eyes. "I got sick of all her drama. She was too clingy. It was fun while it lasted . . . mostly."

"I'm sorry." Remy placed her hand on her friend's.

Emma shrugged. "You win some, you lose some. I just seem to be good at the losing end of things."

A moment of silence passed between the women before Emma spoke. "All right, I'll put the tiny violin away. Let's drink and have a good time. Catch me up on all the gossip."

Mia pulled out her tequila and a few shot glasses. She gave them a lime wedge and salt. "Bottoms up."

Emma smiled and lifted the small glass. "I knew I liked you."

The women downed the liquor and squinted.

"Charli's husband, Finn, has had his deployment overseas extended another couple months," Remy said.

"Who's Charli?" Mia asked.

"The bartender at The Shipwreck. Those two have been sweet on each other since high school," Emma answered.

"That's scary. I hope Finn stays safe," Jasmine added.

"Have you been busy at the bakery?" Mia asked, starting the tamales in the steamer.

"Yes. Wedding season is coming to an end—this is the last month of it. All the fall foliage has some people scheduling events until mid-September. After that, I'll be able to breathe a little easier." Remy sighed.

"How about the inn?"

Jasmine sipped her drink before nodding. "It's been booked solid. All that wedding-season traffic. Thanks for sending them my way, Rem," Jasmine answered.

"How about you?" Remy asked Mia.

"I'm good."

"Come on. Give us the details. I mean, not the dirty specifics because he's my brother and that would be gross," Remy prodded.

Jasmine rolled her eyes. "Now you know how I felt."

Remy smiled with a dreamy look in her eyes before she sighed. "Yeah, but your brother is hot, and amazing, and—"

"Okay, I think that's enough alcohol for this lightweight." Jasmine pulled the margarita from in front of Remy.

"You know, I only seem to drink when we come to Mia's." Remy laughed.

"Well, I'm not related to any of them, so I want the fucking dirty details. Literally." Emma laughed.

"Oh my God." Remy shook her head.

"Karma." Jasmine smiled.

"It's about time Dre had someone good in his life. Tiffany was a bitch," Emma added.

Mia poured herself another shot of tequila, waiting for

the burn to pass before she spoke. "I hate to break it to you, guys, but Dre and I are just friends."

"Friends who fuck," Emma clarified.

Remy covered her face in her hands as if embarrassed.

"Sometimes." Why was she even telling them this?

"You are a fool if you think the way that man looks at you is friendly," Jasmine said.

"Well, it's all I have to offer and he made it clear that's all he wants. Sorry to burst your bubbles," Mia said, taking a gulp of her iced drink. "Come on. Let's bring out this dinner before it gets cold." Mia shut off the burner and removed the tamales, placing the steaming bundles onto a platter.

"I'll go get the guys to help carry stuff," Remy said, wobbling slightly off her stool.

Jasmine laughed. "And I'll help you walk."

"I have a gig at The Shipwreck on Halloween. You should come. It will be fun to dress up, have a few drinks. Bring your man," Emma said, walking over and leaning against the counter next to Mia.

She nodded and forced a smile. "That sounds fun."

October was just a month away—a reminder that this all had to end sooner than later. Her life would be drastically different in the very near future. Would they all hate her after they found out?

Andre and she were destined to fail. He had no grace for liars—even by omission. And she was keeping the greatest secret of all. No, Mia didn't get a happily-ever-after. She had bigger priorities and a promise to fulfill. She'd thought it before, but this time there would be no slipups, no visits to her house under the pretense of helping set up for a party, or bringing takeout. She needed to stop spending time with Andre. It was literally a case of life or death.

Chapter 27

Andre

Ten days. It had been ten strenuous days since he'd been with Mia. It wasn't even just the sex he missed, but her presence and conversation. She had stopped running in the morning. She'd turned him away day after day. The distance between them was widening. His chest ached, like a weight had settled on top of it, getting heavier by the day.

Something was wrong. He ran a hand over his head and let out a frustrated sigh. What could it be?

Panic stole his breath. Could Mia be pregnant? Did she think he'd be angry? Was she not going to keep it? Maybe she didn't need space, but she was just waiting for him to tell her he wanted more. God, he'd been blind. He needed to tell her. The thought of having to live life without her made him sick.

Shit, he loved her!

He'd thought he knew what love was, but he'd been wrong. Nothing compared to how he felt about Mia.

Pressing down on the gas, he sped home from work. Her studio was almost done, Tom was back to work, and everything was right on track. It was time he and Mia were too.

He pulled into her driveway, next to a gray Mercedes with California plates. He walked over to Mia's with a treat from

Remy's café. When he got to the door, he took a deep breath and knocked. Soft steps padded towards him before her silhouette came into view. She opened it and his heart raced. Mia's eyes flashed to his, seeming hesitant. Her hair was pulled back into a sloppy bun, and she had bags under her eyes. She looked exhausted.

"Hey, are you okay?" he asked.

Mia nodded. "Yeah, I'm fine." She didn't budge from the door.

Ask me in.

"I've been meaning to talk to you."

She sighed and rubbed her hand over her face. "I have a headache, so maybe some other time."

"Okay. Sure. Do you need anything?"

Her eyes flashed with some unnamed emotion before she looked away, squeezing the flesh between her eyes over her nose. "I'm good."

Andre held out the bag of pastries. "For when you feel better."

The corner of her lip quirked just the tiniest bit before it was gone so fast he wondered if he'd imagined it.

"Thank you, for everything."

Why did it feel like she meant a lot more than scones? "See you later."

"Bye," she said before closing the door.

He turned around and walked over to his house, the weight still bearing down on his shoulders. He needed a shower. He ran up the stairs and to his room where he tore off his clothes.

Movement from the window caught his attention. Pulling back the curtain, he could see more clearly. A dark-haired man sat on Mia's back porch right next to her. Adrenaline pumped through his veins. His fists clenched. Was she sleeping with him? No. She wouldn't be with someone else. They'd agreed to be exclusive. A whisper of doubt crept into his mind. Would she lie to him? Was this Mia's way of saying it was over?

Fuck.

He went to the bathroom and switched the shower on. Stepping into the water, he didn't even bother to wait until it was warm. Mia wouldn't betray him like that. *But what is that guy doing there if she has a headache?* She was from California, so maybe he was just a friend visiting. *So, why wouldn't she say that?*

After giving himself a quick scrub, he shut it off. He dried and hurriedly pulled on a shirt and a clean pair of jeans, not bothering with boxers. Slipping a pair of sliders on, he walked back to Mia's, unsure of what he would be walking into. But he needed some answers.

He knocked and waited.

Mia opened the door just enough to peek her head out. "Andre?"

"I know you said you were busy, but I need to talk to you about something. Can I come in?"

She hesitated, looking over her shoulder and then back to him while biting her lip. *She still doesn't fully trust me.* What could he do to help her? He'd shown her the most scarred pieces of himself, laying it all bare. Why couldn't she do the same?

"Sure." She opened the door the rest of the way and he walked in, catching sight of not one, but two people.

"Andre, this is my best friend Carmen Lopez, and Mateo," Mia introduced.

Carmen stepped forward and reached out her hand. Andre shook it.

"It's nice to meet you. Are you the man working on Mia's

studio?" Carmen's question was like a tiny arrow piercing his heart.

So, she hadn't told her best friend about him.

"Yeah. And we're neighbors." *And I love her.*

"Oh, wow. This is a small town." Carmen laughed.

Andre's gaze turned to the tall tanned man in the room, nodding. Mateo studied him, looking back and forth between him and Mia. Was he jealous? Mateo moved across the room before taking Mia's hand in his and pulling her into a hug, eyeing him warily. Mia glanced at Andre, offering him a friendly smile as if trying to reassure him.

Had they ever been more than friends?

Andre's fists clenched as his veins burned with jealousy.

Mateo spoke in Spanish as Mia nodded. Andre picked up the words tomorrow, beautiful, and love. Each word was a fucking nail in his coffin. It took everything in him not to snap and unload all his anger onto the guy with his arms wrapped around Andre's woman. Mia was his. Wasn't she?

Carmen cleared her throat, and Andre turned to her. A small knowing smile played at the corner of her mouth.

"I think it's time we go, brother. Let's leave Mia and her guest. We should get back to the inn. We'll see you tomorrow to tour the studio. Mamá will be getting in at noon and we'll be right over from the airport."

Mateo released Mia. "Walk me out?"

Mia glanced to Andre before she nodded. "I'll be right back, Dre."

Andre's eyes remained glued to Mia as she hugged her friends goodbye, leaving a peck on both of their mouths. His knuckles turned white as he watched the exchange between Mia and Mateo.

Mia waved as they drove away before she turned back to the house. She shut the door.

His self-control snapped. "You ever fuck him?"

Mia's glare shot daggers at him, her own anger shining through what looked like fear. "No. We're just friends. He's like a brother to me," she answered, honesty flashing in her eyes. "He's like a brother," she repeated, as if trying to tell him something. "But you have no right to ask me. I really don't have time for your jealousy because I'm not yours and I'm exhausted." She sighed, sitting on the couch. Mia pressed her temples.

He sat next to her, tenderly lifting her face to look at him. "What if I want you to be?"

Mia's eyes watered. Her pulse pounded against his palm. "Mia, I lo—"

Mia's mouth crashed onto his. He groaned from the sudden contact. Her spicy taste cast a spell on him. She guided him to stand and took his hand.

"Mia—"

"Sshhh. No talking. I just need you." Mia pulled his hand and led him up to her bedroom.

He held her face again and kissed her. She sucked, nipped, and caressed his mouth.

I love you. If she wouldn't let him say it, he'd show her with his body.

Slowly, he removed her clothing piece by piece. Her breathing quickened as she reached to strip him as well. Her hands glided across his body, leaving a trail of fire in their wake. He picked her up, her legs wrapping around him. Her pussy was hot against his waist.

Andre laid her on the bed, climbing over her as he used

his mouth to leave a trail of soft sensual kisses down her neck, between her breasts. One hand brushed over her thigh as he sucked her dark nipple into his mouth. She gasped as his hand slid between her legs. She was already wet—ready for him.

She explored his body as he nudged two fingers inside her core. Her legs squeezed around his arm. He moved his mouth to her belly, scratching his beard on her soft responsive skin. She shivered. Andre pressed her knees wider apart before hooking them over his shoulders. He slowly licked her clit as his hands moved in and out of her. She hissed and whimpered, writhing on the bed. Bucking her hips, she cried for more. But he wasn't done devouring her. She tasted so good. He lapped and wiggled his tongue as her legs shook around him. He hummed his approval and she arched her back, lifting off the bed. Sucking her clit into his mouth, he fucked her harder with his fingers, curling them to hit the G-spot. Her inner walls clenched around him as she cried out with her orgasm.

Her body trembled as he returned to slow, savoring licks, not wasting a drop of her essence while she came down from her climax.

Mia greedily reached for him. He sat, pulling his fingers from inside her before he licked them clean.

Her dark eyes filled with lust. Her lips were still swollen from his kiss. A rosy hue coated her cheeks as she swiped her tousled hair behind her ear. Mia pounced on top of him, sending him to his back as she took his hard cock in her hands, moving them up and down. He groaned and clenched his jaw. There was nothing hotter than his cock in Mia's palms.

Mia lowered her head, sucking him into her mouth. *Shit.* He'd been wrong. This was the absolute sexiest image—now burned into his memory. Her swollen lips suctioned up and down his shaft, slowly, torturously. Half-lidded dark eyes stared at him with raw need. He hissed as she took him all the way in, his spine tingling with his impending release. He was gonna come if she didn't stop.

"Mia."

She kept on, her head bobbing, using her tongue to lick the tip before sucking it back into her mouth like a hoover.

Flashes filled his vision as he pulled away from her. "Stop."

She looked at him, questions painting her beautiful face.

"I want to come inside you," he groaned.

"Then take me."

He opened the side drawer and pulled out a condom, but her hand darted out. "You don't need it—unless you want one."

He studied her for a moment. *Is it because she's already pregnant? Or is it because she trusts me?* Either way, he wanted nothing more than to be bare with Mia again.

He dropped the foil packet back into the drawer and climbed on top of her. Their gazes locked as he positioned his cock at her entrance. "Are you ready?"

She nodded and dug her heels into his ass.

Andre thrust inside hard and fast as she sucked in a gasp. He waited until she acclimated before he started moving within her. She closed her eyes, turning her head away.

"Open your eyes. Look at me," he commanded.

She did as tears escaped from the corners of them.

Worry creased his brow. "Are you okay? Do you need me to stop?"

She shook her head. "No. Don't stop. It's because it's so good."

The dam in his chest overflowed—the love he had for this

woman spilling out of him as he rocked her back and forth, making love to her body and soul.

Their gazes locked. He brought her to the brink of pleasure again. He cried out as she tensed around him with her own orgasm. Each nerve ending in his body was alive with euphoria. She had claimed him, every inch, and awakened parts of him he hadn't known existed. And this beautiful creature belonged with him.

The aftershocks vibrated through her before she relaxed beneath him. Reluctantly, he pulled out of her and lay beside her. Tucking her against his chest, he embraced her as she rested her head on him. A few minutes of silence passed as he stroked her hair. The rise and fall of her chest evened out.

"I love you," Andre whispered.

His only answer was her slow deep breaths of sleep.

Chapter 28

Mia

Mia blinked her eyes open. Predawn light filtered in through the window. A heavy arm wrapped around her naked waist and her sensitive parts ached. She'd been too weak and given in. *Again.*

Her eyes burned and she squinted them closed. Andre had said he wanted more. Pain sliced through her heart. The need to create distance between this man she craved and her duty warred inside her. *One more minute.* She'd relish his embrace just a little longer before she faced reality.

Find happiness, mija. But above all else, survive. Her mother's words echoed in her mind. She had to keep her promise to her mother, even if that meant giving up the only thing that made her feel alive.

She carefully maneuvered out from under him. Padding her bare feet over to her dresser, she pulled out the first pair of skinny jeans and blouse she found and shut herself in the bathroom. Mia hurriedly brushed her teeth, got dressed, and threw her hair into a ponytail before sneaking out to her car. She was being a coward, but she couldn't face him today.

Her whole body ached as she drove off towards her friends at the inn. Mia's stomach knotted and flipped the farther away she drove from the man who had captured her heart despite her best efforts.

* * *

Later that afternoon, Mia went to the studio. She could finally breathe again. Whatever discomfort she'd woken up with had begun to lessen. The building smelled of paint and fresh-cut wood, but the lobby was finished. A large custom-built reception desk stood off to the right. She walked through, room by room. Her office was also complete, the walls a sage green with white trim.

Turning around, she headed to the main studio that was almost finished. Tears sprung to her eyes. This was all really happening. Her studio was nearly complete, but with the weight of everything else, the joy she should have felt was diminished. She wiped the tears away.

Why can't I have both love and security? Could it be possible to be happy and safe? Would Andre forgive her for what she'd kept from him? She'd have to tell him everything. If he would listen to her, surely he'd understand why this issue wasn't so black and white. She sniffled, straightening her back. Uncertainty spun through her. She'd never shared all her secrets with anyone before. Could she do it?

I have to. Because I love him.

"Mia."

She jumped and spun around. Andre stood in the doorway, taking up all the oxygen in the room.

Mia forced her lungs to pull in a ragged breath, barely getting enough for a whisper. "What are you doing here?"

He stepped closer, the ache in her body returning with

his proximity. There was no use fighting it—she'd just have to accept that she'd always want what she couldn't have.

"I got worried after I woke to an empty bed. I searched everywhere for you."

"I had to meet my friends. They're leaving tomorrow, but their parents are flying in to see my studio. They should be arriving any minute actually." *And I didn't want to face you.*

Andre reached out, taking hold of her shoulders. "We didn't get to finish our conversation."

"Andre—"

"Tell me what's wrong."

"It's nothing." She waved her hand.

"I need you to be honest with me about something."

She stiffened, her gaze locking with his. *Did he know?*

"Are you pregnant?"

"What?" She frowned. "No! You think I would keep something like that from you?"

"I know I haven't been the most approachable about this whole situation. We got off on the wrong foot and kinda got stuck there for a while. But that changes now. Mia, I love you." He moved his hands to cup her face as a tremble rocked her body. Tears sprang to her eyes.

"I want to wake up to you in my bed every morning. Or, I can stay over at your place." He smiled. "What I feel for you doesn't compare to anything I've ever experienced in my life."

His eyes shone with affection and it was all directed at her. This man loved her. She never thought in a million years she'd fall for someone, and yet, he'd captured her heart so completely. She loved Andre too. But would he still after learning the truth? Could she tell him everything?

Andre's hold didn't waver. He was worth the risk. No

matter what she had to do. This was what her parents had had, and she'd do whatever she needed to hold on to Andre and this once-in-a-lifetime love.

"Mia?" Carmen's voice drifted in through the lobby.

Mia smiled and kissed Andre. "I love you too." *But there's so much you don't know.*

"Mia?" Carmen repeated, poking her head inside the studio. "Oh. There you are. Mamá—"

"There she is!" Mamá Lopez said as she burst in the room past Carmen. Jose and Mateo followed behind her. Andre dropped his arms.

Lucia stumbled forward, Jose reaching out to steady his wife's arm. Mateo gave Mia a sympathetic shrug.

Mamá Lopez grabbed Mia and pulled her into a hug. The smell of vodka burned Mia's nose. A worried knot formed in the pit of her stomach.

"I feared I might never see you again, *mija*. I thought for sure the plane would crash," Lucia said, releasing her.

"The flight attendant thought vodka was a good idea to help calm her down," Jose explained.

"But they didn't take into account Mamá had already had a few drinks before boarding," Carmen added, motioning to her mother.

"Look at you! You're too thin. I need to make you some good food, get sssome meat on those bonesss," Lucia slurred. *Oh, God. Mamá Lucia needs some coffee and food—stat.*

"I promise I've been eating well. I'm just so happy you all could come and see my new studio. Andre here is one of the contractors of the remodel." Mia glanced up at him. He was meeting, for all intents and purposes, the only family she had, drunk or not.

"Andre, this is Lucia and Jose Lopez. They're like my aunt and uncle," Mia explained.

Andre reached out his hand to greet them. "It's an honor."

"Likewise. You've done a great job from what I can see." Jose nodded, studying the space around them.

"It's fantastic, Mia. Your mother would be so proud. You will make the best daughter-in-law. All I ask is for a grandchild sooner than later. *Sí?*" Lucia winked.

Mia's heart leapt to her throat as she snapped her head to Andre's. *Oh, no.*

"I'm sorry. Why would Mia be giving you grandchildren soon?" Andre asked, his tone confused.

Mia's chest burned, too paralyzed with fear to draw in enough oxygen to speak. All the pieces of her carefully crafted story were crumbling before her eyes and she was immobilized with terror to do anything. It was too late to stop it.

Lucia patted her hand over Mia's cheek as she said, "Because my Mia is marrying Mateo next month, of course."

Dre staggered back a step. All the warmth drained from his face. A moment later, anger radiated from him as he glared at her before stalking out of the room.

Her secrets shattered her glass heart into a million pieces.

Chapter 29

Mia

C armen shot Mia a worried look.

"Mamá, let's go see the rest of the place, huh?" Mateo said, quickly coming to her rescue.

Mia ran after Andre, catching up to him before he got in his truck. She grabbed his arm as he swung around, his face masked with fury as the dark storm cloud that hovered above.

"You're engaged to him!"

"Andre, it's not what you think." Her heart pounded. She just needed him to trust her.

"It never is with women, is it?" he snapped.

"I-I can explain." Mia held up her hands, pleadingly.

Andre ground his teeth together, his jaw tense as he glared at her. "Are you or aren't you engaged to him?"

"Yes. But—"

Andre pulled out of her grasp. "That's all I needed to know. You lied to me over and over. If it isn't clear yet, we're done. You should at least tell the sucker you were fucking me behind his back before he signs half his worth over to a liar."

She pushed herself between him and his car. "Andre, please—you said you loved me."

He grabbed her arm firmly and pulled her out of his way. "You were just a good fuck. That's all this was."

"You don't mean that!" Tears streamed down her cheeks as his words eviscerated what was left of her heart.

"Unlike you, I mean what I say," he growled, yanking open the door and climbing in the truck.

"Please, Andre. You know me better than this," she pleaded.

He shook his head. "No, I don't. But whose fault is that?"

The door slammed only a moment before the truck came roaring to life and sped away, taking her heart with it.

She trembled and fell to the ground. Thunder rumbled in the distance. Mia sobbed, her skin prickling with the fire of a thousand tiny paper cuts as the full impact of what happened hit her. She'd lied to stay alive, and traded her soul in the process. No matter the reason, lying was a mortal sin in Andre's book. She'd lost him. Was life worth living alone like this?

A set of arms wrapped around her as she breathed in Mateo's comforting scent.

"Ssshhh. It's okay. I've got you," he said.

Mia stayed like that in his arms until her eyes felt like sandpaper from crying. Standing on shaky legs, Mateo kept his hold on her and kissed her forehead. "Come on. Let's get you home."

Mia searched around. "Where's Carmen and your parents?"

"She took them to get some food in Mamá's belly and sober her up." He guided her to the passenger side of her car.

After buckling in, Mia pressed her temples, seeking relief from the pounding in her head. The ache in her heart compounded the closer they got to her home. Andre was her neighbor—there was no escaping him. The face that had once looked at her with so much affection, would now be permanently filled with disgust.

"I'm sorry about Mamá. You know she's always had it in her head that we'd get married for real. She's just getting impatient for grandbabies."

Mia nodded.

"If you love the guy, then why continue this farce with me? Why not marry him and get your papers that way? It would save me from having to move across the country for a couple years too," Mateo said, parking in her driveway.

Guilt weighed heavily on her shoulders. It had been selfish of her to ask so much of her friend. She turned towards Andre's house.

"I honestly didn't mean to fall in love. It was just supposed to be fun. When I realized . . . it was too late. Andre doesn't forgive liars."

"If you explained to him what was at stake, and if he truly loves you, he'd know there is nothing to forgive," Mateo said, resting his hand on hers.

She sniffed and nodded. "You're right. I need to tell him everything and let him choose." Fear gripped her. Anxiety turned her stomach. *Could she tell him now? Could she expose herself and risk everything? Could she give him the keys to destroy her?*

There was no other choice.

I love him.

She had to try to speak to him, to make him listen—even if that meant risking it all and getting deported back to Mexico.

Even if that meant risking potential death.

Chapter 30

Andre

His chest ached like someone had taken a sledgehammer to it. Anger burned so hot inside him, his skin itched as he tightly gripped the steering wheel.

"Why!" He slammed his fist into the dashboard as searing pain shot up his arm.

Mia lied to me this whole time. He'd been the other man and not even known. *Why does this keep happening to me?* He should have gone with his first instincts. Now his friends would see he was right all along.

Somehow, he made it home.

Andre got out of his car, slamming the door. Glancing at the taut skin on his fist that was swelling quickly, he walked up his porch to the door.

"Dre?"

He whipped around. *This is just not my fucking day. Can't I get a break?*

"Tiffany?" he barked.

The infant in her arms began to wail as she swayed and soothed him. It was another stab to the heart to see her holding the baby that was supposed to be his.

"What the fuck are you doing here?" He didn't have time for games.

Tiffany looked down, tears welling in her eyes as she answered, "He left me—he left *us*."

"Well, you aren't wanted here either." He stuck his key in the door and turned it.

"Please, Andre. I made the biggest mistake treating you like I did. It wasn't until I left that I saw you were the best thing that ever happened to me and I ruined it. I don't know if you can find it in your heart to forgive me."

He shook his head, annoyed. *I can't deal with this too.*

"I just need a place to stay until my sister can get here from Virginia. I don't have a penny to my name. I used the last dollar to come so my son can be safe for a night."

"Guess you should have thought about that before you fucked another man behind my back for a year." He got in his house and slammed the door. The baby outside started screaming again. *Payback is a bitch.* Stalking to the cupboard, he pulled out the bottle of Jack Daniel's and took a big gulp, enjoying the burn of the whiskey. He drank it down until he had to come up for air.

Fuck. Revenge didn't taste as sweet as he'd thought. Even he couldn't be this heartless. *What have I become?*

He stalked to the front door before yanking it open. Tiffany was sitting on the edge of the porch, soothing the baby. She turned to him with watery eyes.

"One night." He turned back to the house, her timid steps following behind. The door clicked shut.

"Can I lay him down in the guest room?" she asked.

He grunted and took another gulp from the bottle.

He lost track of time, focusing on the black label and

dwindling amber liquid. Why couldn't he numb this pain? *Because you love her.*

"Here." Tiffany came in the room with a bag of frozen peas. "For your hand." She placed the cool package onto his swollen knuckles. Rain pelted the roof as thunder rolled.

They sat in the silence as he nursed the whiskey.

"Is this because of me?" she asked.

His eyes snapped to hers. She'd showered and slipped on an oversized men's T-shirt that he didn't recognize. It only fueled his rage.

He shook his head.

"This isn't you, Dre," she whispered.

He laughed bitterly, the room spinning slightly. "She lied to me—just like you did. Only this time, I was the other guy and didn't know it."

"You met someone?"

He brought the bottle to his lips. "And now I need to forget that someone." He took another gulp.

She leaned over, resting her hand on his knee. "Let me help."

Chapter 31

Mia

The pen scribbled across the paper as Mia wrote her life story for Andre to read. She'd never shared these details with anyone, and not even her therapist knew the extent of her trauma. She'd learned from an early age to keep secrets. Exposing herself like this was the hardest thing she'd ever done. Tears leaked from her eyes, blurring the page. She took a deep breath and pulled a tissue from the box.

Her phone pinged and she glanced at it.

Mateo: *If you need our help, let us know. We'll stay in town until tomorrow and then take Mamá and Papá home. Love you.*

Her *familia* had her back, no matter what.

She steeled her spine and put the pen back to the paper, determined to give everything in hopes of earning Andre's forgiveness. Even if they couldn't be together, perhaps it could offer him some relief from the pain he carried inside. She'd seen his scars up close, and never in a million years did she wish to add even a feather more to his burden.

The chorus of raindrops bouncing off the roof brought her a sense of calm and determination. She wrote until her hand ached, her heart bleeding out onto the pages. After folding them and sticking them in an envelope, Mia scribbled his name on it before taking a deep breath.

Mia opened the door as the wind whipped, thunder rumbling nearby. She tucked the envelope close to her chest and darted across the green grass that separated their properties. Taking cover on his porch, she tucked her wild hair behind her ears. Her clothes were covered in dark splotches from the rain as her breath created a small cloud in the cold air. She swallowed, gathering up the courage. She would not take no for an answer. She'd fight for him.

Knocking on the door, she waited.

The door swung open and her heart sank. A beautiful blond woman wearing nothing but an oversized T-shirt opened the door.

"Can I help you?" she asked.

"Um . . . is Andre here?" *Had he found a replacement so soon?* His words came back to haunt her. *You were just a good fuck— that's all this was.*

No. There had to be an explanation for this. Andre wasn't like that. He loved her.

"He's in the shower," the woman answered, studying Mia. *Shower? Did they . . .*

"I can make sure he gets this." The woman reached out to take the envelope from Mia's shaking hand. Her mind was still scrambling to catch up. What did this all mean?

"Who are you?" Mia asked, her stomach churning with anxiety.

"Tiffany. I'm a friend of Andre's."

This was Andre's ex? Why was she here, in his house, half naked? He said he'd loved her too. Maybe he still had feelings for her.

"What the fuck are you doing here?" Andre's voice boomed. He was shirtless, wearing nothing but sweatpants that hung low on his hips.

"I . . ." She blinked back tears.

Tiffany moved out of the way as Andre stood in front of her. He reeked of booze and swayed slightly from side to side.

"I thought I was pretty clear earlier. Stay the fuck away from me." The door slammed in her face. She jumped backwards.

Oh. God. She clutched her stomach, feeling sick. She needed to get away.

Mia ran down the porch onto the road. Her sobs were drowned out by the cracking thunder as the rain soaked her in minutes. Her tears mixed with the fat droplets cascading from the heavens. She ran until her legs and lungs burned—until she crumpled to the ground. It was all too much.

Mamá, I need you. I can't . . .

Emotions overwhelmed her before everything went dark.

* * *

Tap. Tap. Tap. Scribble. Tap. Tap. Tap.

Mia cracked open her eyelids. Everything ached. *Where am I?*

"Oh, good. You're awake."

She turned her head as a young boy's face came into focus. *The boy from the alley!*

She gasped, bolting to a sitting position, every cell punishing her for the sudden movement. She shivered, her clothes soaking wet. She was no longer on the street, but in someone's house. She shifted carefully on the couch, taking in the small living room with a coffee table, chair, and television. A few pictures hung on the wall—artsy photographs.

He held up his hands, dropping the pad of paper and pencil he'd been holding. "I promise I'm not gonna hurt you."

"You're the one from the alley." She held her throbbing head. Her lungs were heavy, making it painful and difficult to breathe.

He reached into his pocket and then held out his palm to her. A glint of gold caught her eye.

My mother's ring!

Mia eyed him warily as she retrieved it.

"I'm so sorry about that. I didn't have a choice. He said . . ."

"I know," Mia croaked. Her throat was raw.

"I stole it back from him and carried it around in hopes of finding you to return it. I couldn't get the necklace though." He stuck his hands in his pockets and shuffled on his feet.

"Thank you . . . Where am I?"

"My sister, Belle's, house. She's a nurse and said you needed to go to the hospital. But we didn't know your name. Found you on the road on our way back from the library."

Mia nodded slowly. "I don't need a hospital. I'll just get going." Mia tried to stand but every muscle protested and the room began to spin.

The boy reached out his hands gently. "Please just rest. I called a friend to come help."

Mia stiffened. "Friend?"

"He's actually the sheriff of Shattered Cove. He's got it bad for my sister, but he's a cool guy. She acts like she hates him, but I think he's wearing her down."

Mia blinked, trying to comprehend everything the boy was saying. Bently was friends with this kid?

"What's your name?"

"TJ. What's yours?"

"Mia."

The floorboards creaked overhead. TJ shifted uneasily. "Uh, I know I don't deserve it, but, uh . . . could you keep that whole thing in the alley between you and me? My sister doesn't know, and neither does Bently."

Before Mia could answer, there was a knock at the door. TJ ran to open it, giving her one more pleading look before he let the visitor with a familiar voice in.

"What's the problem, buddy?" Bently asked.

"I found some lady passed out on the road," TJ answered.

"Mia?" Bently gasped, rushing over to her side just as a beautiful dark-skinned woman came down the stairs in scrubs.

"What is *he* doing here?" TJ's sister snapped.

TJ shrugged.

"Don't act like you're not happy to see me," Bently responded.

She rolled her eyes. "Has hell frozen over?"

Mia would have shaken her head if it didn't hurt so much. Who was this woman, and what did Bently do to piss her off? Her head swam.

"TJ called and let me in. Seems he rescued my friend." Bently turned his attention back on Mia. "What happened?"

"I just need to go home," she rasped, before coughing.

"No, she needs a hospital. Her lungs sound like they have some fluid in them and she's running a fever. She was passed out in the freezing cold, soaked to the bone. No idea how long she was exposed to the elements, but she could have pneumonia," Belle said, crossing her arms.

"Let's go, Mia. Doctor's orders." Bently took her hand as she stood up.

"I'm a nurse," Belle deadpanned.

"Home. No hospital." She coughed again. This time she couldn't stop and everything went black again.

Chapter 32

Andre

*B*ang. Bang. Bang.

"Uhhh," Andre groaned, opening his eyes and immediately regretting it. His head was pounding and whoever was at that door was going to get punched in the fucking face.

Bang. Bang. Bang. Ding-dong. Ding-dong.

"Fuck!" He sat up, swinging his legs onto the ground as empty whiskey bottles clinked and rolled across the floor. Andre rubbed his eyes and got to his feet with the hangover from hell.

Bang! Bang! Bang!

"We're not leaving this time, so you better open the door, fucker, or I'll break it down!" Bently's voice bellowed from outside.

"I'm coming!" he snapped, immediately regretting the loud noise. He went to the door and unlocked it before it swung open, letting in a gust of cool air and two angry sets of eyes glaring at him.

"What the fuck, man?" Bently shoved past him with Mikel following behind.

"What's your problem?" *I need coffee.* Andre shut the door and walked over to start a pot.

"Our problem? He wants to know what our problem is."
Mikel shook his head, joining in with his brother.

The water began to drip, sending the savory rich smell
throughout the kitchen.

"Why haven't you been answering our calls or texts?" Mikel
asked, a little calmer.

"I told you I was sick." And then shut my phone off. "I've
been in bed."

"For a week?" Bently seethed.

"Yeah, must be the flu or something," Andre lied. *Guess
I'm a liar too now.*

"Or a bender," Mikel said, compassion shining from his
eyes.

Bently's gaze softened just a bit. "Maybe he caught it from
Mia."

Her name grated like nails on a chalkboard. How could
those three little letters spark him to life and destroy his soul
all at once?

Andre pulled a mug from his cupboard and poured himself
a big steaming cup of black coffee, not bothering to wait until
it was cool before he took a sip.

"What do you mean I caught it from her?" He couldn't
say *her* name.

Bently shook his head. "You haven't read any of our messages, have you?"

"Nope." He sipped his coffee and took a seat.

Bently and Mikel shared a concerned look.

"What?"

"If you'd answered my calls after you left a message you'd
be out of work this week, you'd have known," Mikel explained.

"Got them, but I told you I needed a week off. You're not

going to play 'bad business partner' on me for skipping out for a few days after you left for five fucking years, are you?"

"Mia was admitted to the hospital a week ago." Mikel narrowed his eyes.

What? Worry sank his stomach like a stone. "Is she okay? What happened?"

Bently sighed and crossed his arms. "She passed out in that storm we had in the middle of the road. Don't know how long she was there before she was found. Luckily, the good citizens called me." Bently raked a hand over his face. "She was in bad shape, man. She passed out again in my arms and I rushed her to the hospital."

He should have been there. Was she all alone? Was her fiancé there?

Crack.

The handle of the coffee mug broke off the cup, and it tumbled and smashed on the counter. He stared at the destroyed porcelain in his hands. *That was the day of our fight.* She'd told him that she blacked out. Why didn't he make sure Mia made it into her house?

Because she shattered what was left of my heart.

"Is she okay?" Andre repeated.

Bently nodded. "She got out yesterday. Wouldn't tell me anything, but begged me not to tell you she was in the hospital. You wanna tell me why?"

Andre set the pieces from the handle on the counter and hung his head. "She lied to me. She lied to all of us. She's been engaged this whole time."

Bently's expression didn't change. Only Mikel seemed shocked.

"Tell me what happened, exactly." Bently took a seat and leaned in on his elbows.

Andre recapped the worst day of his life within a matter of minutes. Both Mikel and Bently shook their heads.

"Just doesn't seem like her," Mikel said.

"Are you *still* taking her side? I was right about her, from the beginning, and you all wanted me to play nice. I should have gone with my gut because look where my fucking heart got me," he snapped.

"Your heart? You love her?" Mikel asked, his brows creased.

Andre sighed. "Fool me twice. She's worse than Tiffany."

"You didn't give her a chance to explain? There's no way she could have duped all of us. There's something fishy about this," Bently said, scratching his beard.

"Nothing hidden here, detective. The guy she's marrying was right in front of me. The same one she'd sworn was like a brother to her. I believed her. She's good at deceiving people. She's a fucking witch who cast us all under her spell."

"Her friend Mateo?" Bently asked.

"You met him?"

Bently nodded. "In the hospital. The whole family stayed for a few days before Mia sent them on their way."

The bastard didn't even stay with her until she was better?

Bently chuckled.

"I fail to see what's so fucking funny here." Andre glared at his friend.

Bently waved his hand. "Mateo Lopez. Tall guy with dark hair, Spanish accent?"

"Yes," Andre grated.

"He's gay. Or, at the very least, bisexual." Bently smirked.

"What?"

"He hit on me. Then when he saw I was a no-fly zone, he got in real cozy with Doc Burton. Saw them at The Shipwreck a few times. They left together both nights," Bently explained.

"Maybe Mateo and Mia have an open relationship?" Mikel suggested.

"Only way you can find out is to talk to Mia." Bently picked up the broken mug and sipped Andre's coffee.

"If I learned one thing through all the shit that went down between Remy and me, it's that you gotta put everything out on the table. I almost lost her because I didn't do that. Don't make the same mistakes I did. If you love her, then hear her out. There has to be an explanation. Do you really want to live the rest of your life wondering?" Mikel asked.

Andre's stomach churned with anxiety. *It hurts too much.* "People don't change."

Mikel winced.

Shit. "I didn't mean it like that. You realize every one of the women I've seriously dated in my life has cheated on me?"

"Mia isn't Tiffany. We all hated your ex. The only reason we were civil was because you really cared for her. We knew she was a bad egg from the beginning. But, Mia . . . she's gotten pretty close with Remy," Mikel said.

"And Jasmine," Bently added.

"You know the girls have better instincts about women than we do. They love her. And your sister is devastated because Mia has been avoiding her this past week." Mikel sighed.

His friends were right. There were more questions than answers. Nothing was adding up. *I need to know.* But would she give him the truth? And how could he trust her even if she did?

Mikel walked over to the couch, sighing. "What's this?"

He reached down and grasped an envelope peeking out from under the coffee table.

Andre shrugged. "Beats me."

"It's got your name on it." Mikel held out the paper.

"That's Mia's writing." Andre reached for it. *How?* Tiffany must have taken it before he shut the door in Mia's face and then stormed to his room.

Bently stood. "Maybe the answers you seek are in there. I'm gonna leave you to it, but I'll be checking back in on you."

His friends said their goodbyes before they left him.

Andre took a deep breath to steady himself as he pulled the folded papers out.

Starting with the first line of the first page, he read.

Each page was harder to digest.

He learned more about Mia in these few pages than he had in the months he'd spent sleeping with her. This was the real Mia. It was no wonder she kept to herself. All the trauma. All the times he'd triggered her by mentioning her parents, or the bad juju that followed her around.

Guilt and hurt swirled inside him as he staggered back to his seat. Humbled, his eyes fell onto the last page.

Chapter 33

Andre

I've lived in fear all my life. It's taken residence in my body, like a shadow following me around. Every decision, every risk I take is weighed based on fear. I realize now that I had pushed you to let go of your resentment and accused you of letting your past hold you back when I have been doing the same. Living life as an undocumented person, losing everyone I ever loved or depended on nearly broke me. I never wanted to risk getting close to anyone else in my life. And then you came along.

I am terrified to be sent back to Mexico to be tortured and murdered like my mother. They fulfilled their threats sent to us each year with her. They sent me pictures. I imagine her last breaths were filled with gasoline and smoke, and the scent of the burning tire around her beaten body. The sad part is, that was the least of the fucked-up things they did to her. I know because they also sent me a letter, and yes, I read it. I forced myself to see what my truth when I was a child did to my parents. I blamed myself for so long. But not anymore. I did not do those things—the cartel did. I can see that now. I will begin the process towards forgiving myself.

I hold DACA status. With the new administration, that status is at risk. I had thought the best thing for me, with limited legal pathways to safety, was through marriage to a citizen. I never lied to you when I told you Mateo and I were like brother and sister. He is my brother, blood or not. I have never, nor will I ever be romantically involved with him. The marriage contract would have been just that—a contract. Mamá Lucia had always hoped we would end up together, but it was never more than a mother's wish. Mateo is not interested in women, and she's still holding on to the dream that he will be someday.

I understand how much I have wronged you. I accept that we can never be. But you should know that I do, and always will, love you, Andre Stone. Beyond that, I trust you with my truth. I've never given that to anyone. The things I've written in these pages could have me deported. But I won't live in fear anymore. I'll face whatever I need to.

My mother told me once that my life was like a piece of sea glass. I'd always taken that to mean it was treacherous, sharp, and unforgiving. But now I see she meant the beauty of it. The unknowing and risk is all a part of our journey—colors and hues sparkling in the panes, reflecting so much beauty if we're willing to see it. Everything we go through refines us, shapes us into who we are.

You helped me realize that. You helped me grow.

Now, I hope you can forgive me, but if not, I'll respect your wishes and leave you alone.

I just needed to let you know the faults made in this relationship were mine.

Don't let my mistakes stop you from finding your happiness.

Yours,

Mia

A weight settled on Andre's shoulders as he read the last of Mia's words. He'd known she had secrets, wondered why she didn't want to report those situations to the police or go to the hospital. If he had seen his parents murdered like that . . . *fuck*.

He'd been blinded by his past hurts, shutting Mia out before she could explain to protect himself. *What have I done?* Because of him, Mia was put in physical danger and had ended up in the hospital. And she had literally risked everything to tell him all of this.

He didn't care that she was undocumented. Why had the system failed her and most likely hundreds of thousands of others? She'd obeyed the laws, her mother had, and look where that had got them.

Andre ran upstairs and got dressed. *I need to make this right.* He brushed his teeth and popped a couple of pain relievers before rushing to get his boots and coat on.

Sprinting across the yard, he sucked in a breath at the sight of the yellow For Sale sign in the front. The thudding in his chest pounded faster as he ran up to her door and banged on it. Her car wasn't there, but maybe . . . He peered in the window. The air was sucked from his lungs. No sign of her. He ran a hand over his hair. *My phone.* He sprinted back to the house. He needed to fix this before Mia disappeared for good.

Chapter 34

Mia

Wiping the sheen of sweat off her brow, Mia walked out of the Hope Facility. The crisp air felt good in her lungs as she headed to her car. After a week in the hospital, she'd been nearly crawling out of her skin. She'd needed to stretch her body. It gave her something to do instead of staying in the lonely hotel room she'd rented to avoid having to see Andre next door. But the gaping hole left in her chest from losing him had pushed her to reach out for a lifeline. The moment he'd mentioned this place, her soul had been tugged in this direction. Children with pasts she could relate to, with a need for an outlet. Yoga had helped her, so why not them?

Aaron had been delighted and gathered the kids together not thirty minutes after she'd introduced herself. *Too bad it's only temporary.* She couldn't stay here—but Shattered Cove had become her home. Her business was here. She'd made friends. Mia winced and reached for her phone. A slew of unanswered and unread text messages sat in her inbox. *I doubt they'll still want to be my friend. Not after they learn the truth.*

She wouldn't put them in the middle of her and Andre. He'd obviously wanted nothing else to do with her. She understood his reasons, but it didn't make it hurt any less. Anger boiled at the visual of his ex in his house. Why would he take her back like that? Maybe he still harbored feelings for her and Mia had been blind this whole time.

She sighed and slipped into her car. Not ready to go back to her lonely hotel room.

Remy and Jasmine deserved the truth, even if their friendship was doomed.

She clicked open her messages.

Mikel: *Renovations are complete. Let me know when you want to do the final walk-through.*

He'd been the only one she'd remained in contact with, and just because he stayed professional—his content was strictly about her studio.

Mia: *I can meet you this afternoon. Does 2 p.m. work?*

Her phone buzzed a moment later.

Mikel: *See you then.*

Mia clicked open Remy's messages next. Remy had come to the hospital, but Mia had avoided talking too much, using her sore throat as an excuse—an exaggeration, but still true. Remy had shown up for three days in a row with homemade soup, frowning at what the hospital provided. Mia hadn't been hungry, but she'd made an effort for her friend. Eventually Mia had to shut her out too and ask her not to come back.

Remy, being the good friend she was, had swallowed the hurt that flashed in her eyes and did as Mia asked.

Remy: *Let me know if I can bring you anything. Please, Mia. I really care about you. You're my friend no matter what is going on between you and my brother—and friends help each other.*

Remy: *Mia, Bently said you've been out of the hospital for days now. Where are you? I swung by the house, but it's all packed up. Please don't leave like this. Let me in.*

Yes, her house was for sale. She couldn't bear another minute being so close to the man she loved who probably hated her now. Thankfully, money made the world go around. The real estate agent who'd helped her close on her house was more than happy to help her sell. She'd hired another company to pack, move, and store her things. She only kept a few suitcases with her essentials at the hotel.

Remy: *Mia? I don't know what else to say. Dre isn't responding . . . and you're freezing me out. I'll be here when you're ready to talk.*

Mia blinked back tears. Was there no end to the grief that leaked from her eyes? She pulled open the messages from Jasmine.

Jasmine: *Remy is going crazy over here. Look, I know enough about secrets to see you have them. But you and Dre are so good for each other. Please come back. We don't have to talk about it. We can pretend like nothing happened, but I miss you, Mia. I don't say that to many people.*

A pang of guilt shot through her chest. *What have I done?*

She typed a group text to her two friends: *Hey, guys. I'm sorry I've been a ghost. I'm ready to talk if you still want to. I'm meeting Mikel at the studio at 2, so maybe we can meet up there afterwards?*

The studio would be a neutral place. No chance of meeting Andre there because surely, he would be avoiding her too.

She had three missed calls from him and one voicemail. Pain stabbed her heart. She couldn't handle listening to that right now. Maybe later with a bottle of tequila. What could he possibly have left to say to her? Nothing good, that was for sure. Mia put her phone down. She'd catch up on the rest of her messages another time.

She drove towards her new business, her happiness for the finished product clouded by a fog of regret.

* * *

At 1:45, she opened the door with her key. The smell of fresh paint still lingered. Not waiting for Mikel, she drank in the silence as she walked from room to room. Memories of Andre haunted each one. He was a part of this place, as much as she wished she could forget him.

Her chest squeezed and she hugged her arms around herself. She was alone. Again. On her own.

Making her way into the main studio, she surveyed the large room. Mia gasped, clamping her hand over her mouth. The wall she'd wanted torn down had a giant window made from what looked like sea glass. The sun shone through it, sending a rainbow of colors swirling all over the gleaming wood floor. She stepped into the light, reaching out as the hues dappled her hand. Tears slid down her cheeks. *It's perfect.* This was the embodiment of her mother front and center— her dream come true. *Mamá, you're here. Aren't you?* The colors danced across her skin, warming as her mother's spirit surrounded Mia with love.

"I thought you'd like it, to remember your mom."

Mia startled and spun around.

Andre walked forward, his hands in his pockets. She wiped the tears from her eyes and caught her breath. Searching his face, she saw no trace of the disgust or anger she expected from him. Andre's expression was tired, and unreadable otherwise.

"You did this?" she managed.

He nodded and stopped a foot in front of her. "I know a guy. When you decided to go with a window, and then I overheard you and Lyra talking about how she used to collect sea glass . . . I wanted to surprise you."

"Thank you."

A moment of silence followed as Mia studied him for any sign as to how to proceed. His expression morphed to pity and she backed up a step, dropping his gaze. That's what this was. *He just feels bad for the poor little girl who lost her parents.*

"Mia?"

She winced, her name so tender from his lips, like he still loved her. "Are you here to do the walk-through? I thought Mikel—"

"No." He stepped closer.

"I'm sorry, Andre. I . . ."

"I'm sorry too."

Her eyes snapped to his. "What do you have to apologize for? I deserved your reaction."

He shook his head and reached out his hands to cup her face. She closed her eyes, fighting off a wave of fresh tears. Energy hummed between them, sparking to life with the touch of his hands. He was so gentle with her, as if she was the one made of glass.

"Mia? Look at me," he pled.

She opened her eyes, her heart too afraid to hope, her knees weak and wobbling.

"I should have given you the chance to explain." He swallowed. "After reading your letters, I understand why you kept so much inside."

She blinked a tear away as he brushed it from her cheek with his thumb.

"I'm honored that you shared all of that with me."

She nodded, not trusting her voice. A swirl of emotion twisted up inside her like a tornado. Fear. Love. Grief. Happiness. Guilt. *Hope.*

"I thought I knew what love was. I figured I got one shot at it and had wasted it on my ex."

She winced.

He pulled her closer. "But I was so wrong. Because I fell into a love so deep it scared me. It snuck up on me slowly. I didn't realize until I was consumed by it. So, when I thought . . . I ran like a coward because I was afraid of being hurt again. You destroyed me."

Pain laced through her heart. "I'm—"

His finger laced across her lips, shushing her. "Then your words in that letter, they rebuilt me."

What was he saying?

"You helped make me stronger. You challenge me in so many ways." He smirked. "And I love every minute of it."

But do you love me?

He leaned in, his mouth brushing softly against hers, sending a rush of heat throughout her body. Her yearning was held back by a thread of doubt.

"I love you, little witch. You've captured me—every part is yours."

He loved her! She gripped his shoulders, not willing to let this moment disappear. She pulled him closer and kissed him hard.

He leaned his forehead against hers as she caught her breath.

"What about *her*? Why was she at your house? Did you . . ." Her stomach churned.

"God no. She showed up because her boyfriend left her and she needed a place to stay for the night. Nothing happened—despite her attempts. I couldn't . . . . I'd never."

"You don't still have feelings for her?" Mia clarified.

"No." His answer was absolute. "I love *you*. There's no room for anyone else."

Relief flooded over her like a crashing wave. She slanted her mouth across his. "I love you too."

"Marry me instead of Mateo," he said.

She froze. Stunned, she backed her head away to look him in the eyes. "No."

His brows creased together as he frowned. "What?"

"I'm not marrying you for a green card."

"Then marry me because I want to spend the rest of my life with you. Marry me so we can start a family together someday. Marry me because I love your stubborn ass, damn it." He nearly growled his last words and palmed her backside.

She couldn't stop the smile that formed on her lips. "We've only known each other for a few months."

"I know all I need to know about you. This is me, showing you I trust you. I'm offering you my heart. I promise to love you, to never walk away from you when you need me, and to be loyal always. I want to be your partner in life. I want to share all the ups and downs we're very likely to have based on our tempers."

She laughed.

"I want you, forever." He searched her eyes. "Do you want that too?"

She searched his eyes in return, and found nothing but genuine love reflecting back. Life was temporary. But perhaps love didn't have to be. Her mother had always told her, sometimes you just had to have faith that things would work out. That there'd be a rainbow after the storm.

"*Si, mi amor. Siempre.* Forever."

Andre's mouth crashed onto hers as he lifted her into his

arms. She held on to him, his love and forgiveness overpowering and staggering. She kissed him back with everything she had in her, trying to show him how much she wanted this. Lips fused, tongues reconnected, and she got lost in him. Bliss wound around her like warm sunshine lighting her up from the inside out. She was getting her fairy tale after all.

A throat cleared somewhere in the room.

She broke the kiss and turned. Mikel walked towards them, Bently, Jasmine, and Remy behind him.

Andre set her back to her feet as she straightened her shirt, heat flooding her cheeks.

"Looks like that went well." Bently smirked.

Mia glanced at Andre, questioningly.

"I've been looking for you. I enlisted their help."

Do they know?

"I didn't tell them the details, only that you had good reasons for doing what you did. And it is your secret to tell if you want," he said low enough for only her to hear, as if he'd read her mind.

She blinked, nearly blinded by the overwhelming adoration she felt for this man. Her heart was bursting at the seams.

"Thank you." She turned to the group of friends that had become more like family in Shattered Cove. "I owe you all an explanation for my recent behavior."

Epilogue

Mia

One year later

The sunlight glinted off the selenite engagement ring on her finger next to her mother's gold wedding band. She'd found her happily-ever-after after all. Once she'd told Andre about the meaning behind the selenite in connection to her mother, he understood why she wanted it in the foundation of her studio. That was something they'd worked on for the last twelve months—communication and building trust. And now she had something even bigger to communicate to her husband—something that would change them forever.

"*Buenas tardes, hermosa.*" Andre's deep voice rumbled behind her.

She turned as he walked into the studio.

"Good afternoon to you too, husband." She smiled and wrapped her arms around him. "Did you lock the front door behind you?"

"Yes. Are you ready to go home?"

Home. She'd never get tired of hearing that from the love of her life. "Not yet. I have something to do first."

"Oh yeah?" His eyebrows rose as he smiled suggestively

and lowered his hands to her ass. "How about we peel down these leggings and I make you come against that wall again?"

"Mmm. That sounds like a fantastic idea."

He pulled her hand and led her over to the wall. Pushing her back to the surface, he pressed kisses around her face, ending on her lips. His hands moved the edges of her pants down her legs as he dropped to his knees.

"Dre?"

"Yeah, baby?" He licked his lips and dipped his fingers into the slick folds of her pussy. The bolt of electricity shocked her core as it always did when he touched her.

If he only knew how fitting his words were.

"I hope you lied to me that day you professed your love and asked me to marry you."

He stopped, withdrawing his hands and standing to his feet. "What?"

"You said you only had room in your heart for me."

"Yeah . . ." he said, his attention locked on her.

"I hope you have room for someone else too." She bit back a smile.

"What are you talking about?"

She placed his hand over her belly. "I'm pregnant, Andre."

The stunned look only lasted a minute before the biggest grin she'd ever seen graced his face. "We're gonna have a baby? I'm going to be a dad?"

She nodded, her own joy uncontainable. She'd never imagined she'd be secure enough in life to have this.

He kissed her hard. "We're having a baby!"

She laughed. Her heart was so full of light and love. There, under the splatter of color from the sea glass window, she had a child growing in her womb and her husband by her side with nothing but pure love shining from him.

The sadness for her parents' absence would always be there. Some days were easier than others. But Mia would make sure her mother's spirit would live on through her, and now her child.

"I think we should celebrate," Andre said, dropping to his knees again.

"With orgasms?" she asked, as his skilled fingers dove inside her, finding her G-spot.

"All the orgasms," he agreed before lowering his face to her, and true to his word, he delivered several orgasms until she saw nothing but the rainbow of colors blurring her vision.

Somehow the broken, jagged pieces of her heart had been smoothed and strengthened over time like sea glass, until all that was left was the beauty and joy. She'd always carry her trauma with her, but she'd learned how to live her life without it defining her.

"I love you, Mia."

"I love you too." *Forever.*

Now, turn the page for a sneak peek of Book 3 of The Shattered Cove Series, *Defying Gravity* (Bently and Belle's story) right now.

Sneak Peek of *Defying Gravity*

Chapter 1

Bently

Bently winced at the bitter aftertaste coating his mouth. He lifted his cup of coffee and swallowed again. Nope. Still terrible. "Should have stopped by Remy's," he said aloud to the empty truck cab as he set the brown sludge passing for java in the cup-holder.

The radio crackled. "Squad one, what's your twenty and status?"

Bently picked up the radio as he turned into a side street and pressed the speaker to his mouth. "This is squad one. I'm on Everton Street. Status ten-eight."

"Unit one, take the suspicious person walking with a bike on Shell Ave."

He pressed the button once more. "Ten-four."

Bently put his blinker on and went left at the stop sign, scanning the sides of the road. After making a series of turns, he ended up on Shell Avenue. Slowing, his gaze focused on a kid pushing a bike on the side of the road. His blue school backpack was nearly bursting at the seams. Bently scanned the upscale neighborhood for any signs of a threat.

"He's just a kid walking home from school." He shook his

head and notified dispatch that he was on the scene before pulling up beside the kid.

He hopped out. Squinting at the sun, he grabbed his aviators from his pocket and slipped them on as he greeted the kid. "Good afternoon."

The teen kept walking with his head down, swaying slightly. The flapping of deflated rubber slapping against the cement sidewalk brought Bently's attention to the tires of his bike.

Bently stepped next to the boy. White earbuds stuck out of his ears, contrasting with his light-brown skin. He moved into the young man's periphery to get his attention. "He—"

Wide frightened brown eyes stared up at him as the boy's trembling hands flew towards the sky. The bike crashed to the ground. Bently swiveled around searching for the danger that had the guy so riled up, but they were alone on the street.

"Sir, I don't want any trouble. I'm just walking home from school." The young boy's voice was steady. His eye was swollen and bruised.

Bently furrowed his brow. *He's scared of me?* Smiling in hopes to set the boy at ease, Bently motioned to his headphones. "Can you take those out for a minute?"

Slowly, the boy plucked the headphones from his ears, the steady thump of hip-hop pouring from the tiny speakers.

"Nice tunes." *Smooth, Bently.*

The young man remained silent. His eyes were glued on Bently. His shoulders nearly touched his ears with tension.

"I'm Sheriff Evans. What's your name?"

"TJ . . . uh, Thomas Jones, sir."

Bently nodded, looking over his bike. "What happened to your ride?"

TJ looked down for a moment before he shrugged. "Flat tire."

"May I?" Bently asked, reaching towards one of the wheels.

"Okay?" TJ's answer was more like a question.

"I know a thing or two about bikes. This is a nice one."

"I didn't steal it if that's what you're thinking," TJ said, his jaw tense.

"I never assumed you did. You can put your hands down you know." Bently ran his palm around the outer tire, finding the source of the leakage—a long slice between the folds of black rubber.

"The person who slashed these tires the same one who gave you that black eye?" Bently asked, standing to his full height.

TJ shifted nervously. "Why do you care?"

Bently sighed. "Because this is my town and I care about the people in it. If someone is being harassed or assaulted, I want to know."

TJ nodded hesitantly.

"Do you want to file a report?"

TJ's eyes grew wide again as he shook his head vehemently. "Nah, it was just a misunderstanding."

"If you're sure." Bently knew better than anyone else that you couldn't help someone until they were ready to be helped.

A flash of movement caught his eye. One of the residents stared out the window of her two-story home at him, her hand clutching the fabric of her shirt.

"Where do you live?"

"Maple Street."

"That's still two miles away. Why don't you hop in and I'll give you a ride? I'll throw your bike in the back." Bently picked up the metal frame.

"You don't have to," TJ said.

"Wouldn't want you to have any more misunderstandings on the way back. Besides, I'm headed that way anyway. I have a friend who lives in that neighborhood." *And the last thing I need is another phone call to dispatch about a kid walking home from school. Since when did that become a crime?* "Would you like the ride?"

"Uh . . . okay." TJ opened the passenger side and climbed in.

Bently hefted the bike into his truck bed before climbing in the driver's side. Geez. Had anyone ever sat farther away from him and still managed to be in the same car? The kid was practically crawling out the window.

He wasn't blind. The kid was terrified of him, and unfortunately, Bently guessed the badge across his chest had something to do with it. There were so many news stories, seemingly a story everyday about clashes of police and people of color. How could Bently assure him that wouldn't happen here in Shattered Cove? He was not a racist, and no one in his department was either—at least he didn't think so. Maybe he should slip in the fact that his sister-in-law was black? No, that'd be awkward.

"You play any sports?" Bently drove towards their destination.

"Basketball."

"Oh, my kind of guy . . . You lived here long?" Bently tried to keep the strain out of his voice.

"Since August. My sister got a job at the hospital."

"What about your parents?" Bently turned down the end of the street.

"It's just us. There, the blue one on the right is ours." TJ pointed out the window to a small duplex. The burlap wreath over the door said 'welcome'.

Bently pulled in along the side of the street and put the truck in park. TJ hopped out, quickly shutting the door, and Bently followed suit. He walked around to the back to grab the bike just as a door slammed behind him.

"Oh, shit," TJ said.

"What the hell happened to your face TJ?" A strong feminine voice growled.

Bently turned. The breath ripped from his lungs. The woman before him was the most beautiful person he'd ever laid eyes on—and he'd laid eyes on a lot. Big ringlets of curls danced around her brown glowing skin in the breeze. Her dark eyes flashed at TJ with worry before she targeted him with those stormy spheres. Fear tinged the edges of her furious glare. Her bright red lips moved as his ears rang, blood rushing to his groin.

"Did he do this to you?" She grabbed TJ's face, checking him over like a mother hen. TJ turned away from the unnamed beauty.

"Nah, just some kids at school messing around," TJ said. "Sheriff Evans gave me a ride."

"You got in the car with a cop?" she snapped.

Bently closed his mouth, embarrassed that he'd been standing there gawking. Wiping invisible drool from his mouth, he cleared his throat and extended his arm, offering the smile that he'd been told melted most women's panties. "Hi. I'm Bently."

She stared at his open hand like he'd just stuck it in a public toilet. "Is my brother in any trouble?"

He frowned and straightened from the rejection. "No. Of course not."

"Good, then we're done here." She grabbed TJ's arm and pulled him into the house while Bently stared, utterly confused. *What the hell just happened?*

"Belle! My bike——" TJ protested.

"Get inside!" His sister shot him a look and TJ shut his mouth and complied.

It needs the tires fixed anyways. I can do that.

The woman shoved her brother in the house and whirled around. Her powerful gaze met his before she slammed the door shut.

Damn, she was something.

* * *

A few hours later, Bently pulled the bike from his truck bed, admiring his handiwork. This fresh set of tires and the tune-up he'd performed would be the perfect icebreaker. It wasn't unusual for him to go above and beyond the call of duty for his fellow townsfolk. But none of them had a sister who was hotter than sin and feisty as fuck either. *Does this count as breaking my no-hooking-up-with-locals rule?*

Nah. This was just good old-fashioned flirting and helping a fellow community member out. It wasn't like he would follow through.

Bently knocked on the door, noting the older model Ford Focus in the driveway that had seen better days. Red flowers bloomed at the base of the porch, a discarded pile of pulled weeds off to the side. Several potted plants were spaced around the small area and a few baskets hung from the rafter hooks. He swiped the sweat from his brow and drew in a deep breath. Nerves scattered through him as he shifted his feet. Since when was he this off kilter over a woman?

The energy shifted as the knob twisted. His heart beat faster as he swallowed.

The door opened and Belle's smile quickly morphed into a frown.

"What do you want?" Belle said, her chin rising.

"Good evening." He smiled and waited a beat. Her scowl only deepened. *Have I lost the touch? Did cancer steal this from me too?* He cleared his throat. "Uh, I just wanted to return TJ's bike."

She looked at the metal object as he set it on the porch. "Okay."

"Is he home?"

"He's doing homework," she answered with a hint of suspicion in her voice.

"I'll only be a second. If you don't mind, can I come in and ask him about who gave him that shiner one more time?" *Maybe she'll see I'm just trying to help.*

"Do you have a warrant?"

"E-excuse me?" he asked, baffled. He was used to not being everyone's favorite person as an officer of the law, but this was something more.

"Unless you have a warrant, you cannot come into my house or search my property. I know how *you people* work."

What the fuck?

"You leave my brother alone. He's smart and he's going places. He's a good boy. We don't want any trouble, *officer*." Belle's voice was steady, but her trembling hand gave it away. He glanced at her dainty fingers shaking at her side.

Belle balled them into fists before he considered her face, the fear in her eyes. *She's scared of me.*

"I never intended to cause trouble. Just wanted to make

sure he got home safe. Have a good evening, ma'am." He turned and walked back to his truck, utterly speechless.

Defeated, he started the engine and shifted into gear. He needed a good strong drink. A woman's company wouldn't hurt either. Visions of sucking on those red lips and fisting those dark curls made his cock jerk. He gripped the steering wheel until his knuckles turned white.

Too bad it would only be a fantasy and his hand tonight.

To continue reading Bently and Belle's story, visit the website below to get your copy.

www.amkusi.com/defyinggravity

Thank You

Thank you for reading *Glass Secrets*. We hope you are emotionally satisfied with Andre and Mia's love story. If you enjoyed this novel, please consider leaving a review on your favorite retailer and sharing it with your friends and family.

Also, you can get book 3 in *The Shattered Cove Series* right now!

Bently and Belle in ***Defying Gravity (Book 3)***.

Thank you again for reading Glass Secrets!

Cheers,
Ash & Marcus.

About A. M. Kusi

A. M. Kusi is the pen name of a wife-and-husband team, Ash and Marcus Kusi. We enjoy writing romance novels that are inspired by our experiences as an interracial/multiethnic couple.

Our novels are about strong women and the sexy heroes they fall in love with, are emotionally satisfying, and always have a happy ending.

Discover more about us at:

www.amkusi.com

To receive updates about new releases, preorders, give-aways, and more, visit the website below to join our newsletter today:

www.amkusi.com/newsletter

After you join the newsletter, we will send you a FREE novella to read.

To contact us, use this email address:

amkusinovels@gmail.com

Happy reading!
Ash & Marcus

Also by A. M. Kusi

Choose your next read from these series and standalone novels today.

A Fallen Star
(Book 1 in The Shattered Cove Series)

Defying Gravity
(Book 3 in The Shattered Cove Series)

The Orchard Inn
(Book 1 in The Orchard Inn Romance Series)

Conflict of Interest
(Book 2 in The Orchard Inn Romance Series)

Her Perfect Storm
(Book 3 in The Orchard Inn Romance Series)

For a complete list of all our books, visit:
www.amkusi.com/books

Made in the USA
Middletown, DE
23 April 2021